ADVANCE PRAISE

"As slick as a switchblade with a pearl handle."

— **Lee Child**, the *New York Times*-bestselling author of the Jack Reacher novels

"This brief novel crackles with sharp dialogue—"if you can't lie to your wife, who can you lie to?"—and a witty narrative voice that puts the reader in mind of Elmore Leonard....This one could make it to the big screen, but don't wait for the movie. Buy the book. It may be the first of a long series."

— ***Kirkus Reviews*** STARRED REVIEW

"I loved this book, with its myriad twists and turns. It has the pace of an action movie and the humor we've come to expect from Phoef Sutton."

— **Bob Newhart**, actor and author of *I Shouldn't Even Be Doing This*

"*Crush* reads like Elmore Leonard on crack...a nonstop thrill ride of a crime novel that's packed with action, smart-ass dialogue, colorful characters, and one harrowing plot twist after another. This novel will leave you breathless...and aching for the sequel."

— **Lee Goldberg**, author of *The Heist* and *The Job* (with Janet Evanovich), *The Walk*, and many other thrillers

"Filled with snappy dialogue and sarcasm, but also mixed with a genuinely intriguing storyline."

— ***Over My Dead Body***

"Sutton is the rare storyteller who writes with amped speed, laugh-out-loud humor, and utter suspense. *Crush* deserves to be a smash."

— **Bruce Feiler,**
New York Times-bestselling author

"In Caleb Rush, Sutton has created an iconic L.A. character—funny, violent, smart, broke, surrounded by lowlifes and minor celebrities—and zapped new life into a classic genre. How many Crush novels do I want to read? As many as Sutton writes."

— **Rob Long,** host of NPR's Martini Shot
and award-winning television writer

"A fast-paced, hard-hitting novel layered with mystery, muscle, and heart."

— **Reed Farrel Coleman,**
New York Times-bestselling author
of *Robert B. Parker's Blind Spot*

"This book never pauses, never quits, and its hero slows down only long enough to reload. Reading it is like holding a burning firecracker in your hand. Much safer to toss it away, but where's the fun in that?"

— **Nick Griffin,** screenwriter of
Matchstick Man and *Terriers*

"As necks snap, lies fester, and mercies scoff, the uncaged beasts in Sutton's wildly sly debut novel *Crush* leave L.A. a time-shared Hades. Fluent in the wicked lowdown, the novel's dizzying poisons mount, its characters a deadly, deranged splendor. The violence is cinematic, and Sutton's infrared wit kills."

— **Richard Christian Matheson,**
bestselling author of *Dystopia* and
screenwriter of many horror
films and television shows

"Phoef Sutton has created a character who's impossible not to fall in love with, in a story that moves like a bullet train through the mean streets of L.A. If you're anything like me, you'll be begging for a sequel the moment you turn the last page."

— **Robert Gregory Browne,**
bestselling author of the Trial Junkies series

"A witty, irreverent, and sexy thrill ride through the famous guts of Los Angeles. Sutton writes his characters in great splashes of color, stirs them into a whirlwind, and releases them into his world with glorious results."

— **Richard Ellis Preston, Jr.,** author of
The Chronicles of the Pneumatic Zeppelin series

"Sutton crushes it in *Crush*, a nonstop action thriller. If you like Jack Reacher, you'll love *Crush*."

— **Joel Goldman,** author of *Stone Cold*
and *Chasing the Dead*

"*Crush* hits you with all the power and speed of a maniac wielding a baseball bat. If you ever need anyone to take out Jack Reacher, Caleb 'Crush' Rush is your guy. An action-filled, finger-snapping romp."

— **Paul Bishop,** LAPD detective
and author of *Lie Catchers*

"Sutton's *Crush* is what would happen if *The Friends of Eddie Coyle* went out for a night of drinking and fighting. Snappy dialogue, sharp writing, and righteous violence."

— **Jay Stringer,**
author of the Eoin Miller trilogy

"*Crush* takes the reader on a dizzying carnival ride through the mean streets of L.A. Rush is an ass-kicker from the Patrick Swayze *Roadhouse* school of self defense."

— **W.L. Ripley,** author of the Cole Springer
and Wyatt Storme mysteries

"Like a gunshot, *Crush* starts with a bang, whizzes by at a breakneck pace, and hits its mark with precision. The setting feels like the real underbelly of L.A., and Sutton's humorous touches crackle with energy. It reads like you're watching a modern film noir. It's a cliche to say that I couldn't put it down, but that's what happened. I was riveted from start to finish."

— **Bill D'Elia,** director of *Boston Legal*
and *How to Get Away With Murder*

"If you enjoy reading novels peopled by soulful characters forever taking their own psychic pulses, then *Crush* is not for you. If, on the other hand, you like hard-boiled crime fiction with a narrative line propelled by startling twists and turns and relentless action, then you won't want to miss this book. That action in *Crush* literally defines 'nonstop,' and the eponymous protagonist does the same thing for the term 'heroic.' I couldn't put it down till I arrived at the tangled, violent conclusion. Phoef Sutton has a winner."

— **Tom Kakonis,** author of
Treasure Coast and *Double Down*

"Check out *Crush*, a hilarious novel by Phoef Sutton. A cross between Elmore Leonard and Donald Westlake, Sutton is a real find. Prepare to laugh away the night."

— **Robert Ward,**
author of *Red Baker* and
Four Kinds of Rain

ALSO BY PHOEF SUTTON

Wicked Charms (with Janet Evanovich)

15 Minutes to Live

Reborn: A Dead Man Adventure
(with Kate Danley and Lisa Klink)

The Dead Man: Midnight Special

BY PHOEF SUTTON

Published by Prospect Park Books
2359 Lincoln Avenue
Altadena, California 91001
www.prospectparkbooks.com

Distributed by Consortium Book Sales & Distribution
www.cbsd.com

Library of Congress Cataloging-in-Publication Data
Sutton, Phoef.
Crush / Phoef Sutton. -- First edition.
pages ; cm
ISBN 978-1-938849-36-7 (softcover)
I. Title.
PS3569.U896C78 2015
813'.54--dc23
2014041275

Cover design by Howard Grossman
Book layout and design by Amy Inouye
Printed in the United States of America

CRUSH
A NOVEL

To Lee Goldberg; he knows why

ONE

The first time Amelia saw him, she didn't think of him as a person so much as an obstacle. Cold eyes and muscles, he was standing in a corner of the club, like a piece of the furniture. Only larger.

The bouncer. The immovable object. No need to wonder why they called him Crush—his hands looked like they could squeeze the air out of her windpipe in a second.

The club was called the Nocturne. On the intersection of Melrose and Clinton. It was one of those nightspots with no sign out front, so you had to be cool enough to know about it to even know about it. Inside, all was darkness and colored lights and blaring music. Gorgeous young girls and buff young boys trying to convince themselves they were having the time of their lives. The décor was blood red and velvet—Queen Victoria meets Sacher-Masoch—with walls upholstered in brass-studded scarlet leather. The bar itself was a mahogany monstrosity that the owner lifted from some

Gold Rush ghost town. It dwarfed the pretty bartender behind it, but Crush, stationed at the east end, was big enough to make even that huge bar look pint-size. In his black T-shirt, fit tightly over his bulging muscles, he faded into the décor, not blending in with the wall but looking like he *was* the wall. His clean-shaven head had a nasty scar running from above his left eye, across his skull, to the back of his neck, like a racing stripe. Only his startling blue eyes made Amelia think that there was a human being behind the barrier. Crush made no extraneous sounds or movements. Like a good bouncer, he made sure you didn't notice him unless he wanted you to.

◎

The bouncer's eyes took in everything that was going on around him. The gangbangers at the back booth, pounding Cristal. The blonde with the hungry eyes sitting by the bookshelf filled with prop books. The underage boy hitting on the underage girl under the chandelier. The bone-thin network exec and her wing woman at the banquet, trolling for love. The hooker by the men's room, also trolling for love, though she didn't know it. The sad drunk at one end of the bar, lost in the world of his shot glass. The confident loser at the other end of the bar, chatting up the bartender as she topped off his mojito. The Latina girl with the God-given ass, attracting too much attention on the dance floor for her boyfriend's comfort. Crush's eyes saw them all and gauged their potential for trouble, like a gamer watching the life-bars over characters in a video game.

The guy hitting on the bartender did a drumroll on the bar and said he'd be right back after he drained the snake.

The bartender sighed, watching him go. "Five years ago, I was so pretty that guys like that were afraid to talk to me," she said to Crush. "Now I'm just pretty enough that guys like that *want* to talk to me. I hate that."

Crush nodded but didn't answer. He and the bartender had the kind of friendship that meant they didn't have to talk. That's the kind of friendship he liked.

Crush had a real name (it was Caleb Rush), but not many people used it. The bartender had a name, too, Catherine Gail. It was Gail who got Rush the job at the club. She was in her mid-thirties, with long black hair shot with a streak of gray, sharp features that got better with age, and a magnificent scar on her lower lip that made men want to take her home and marry her.

Gail was a taekwondo master "slash" bartender. Everybody was a "slash" something these days, Rush reflected. Who could get by on just one job? He himself had several. It was a "slash" kind of world out there.

Rush had gone through quite a few martial-arts teachers in his day. He picked things up quickly, so the instructors loved him at first. Then they'd get threatened and try to kick his ass. That wasn't a good idea. Rush had hurt a lot of martial-arts teachers.

But with Gail it was different. She was calm, wise, centered, and very Zen. Sort of like a hot version of Master Splinter from the Ninja Turtles. And Rush worshipped her. To most people, he seemed a tough man, but he was humble and obedient when he found someone he truly respected. That had happened once or twice in his thirty years. Those thirty years had been spent in odd ways, doing odd things. Many of them were things that Rush would rather forget.

On the dance floor, the girl with the God-given ass was displaying her gift a little too aggressively, and one of the other dancers was staring at it—he'd have taken a bite out of it if it had stopped moving long enough for him to get his teeth on it.

All at once, God-given Ass's boyfriend was in front of the other guy, claiming his turf. "Are you looking at my girl's butt?!"

"It's looking at me! That butt's calling my name!"

The boyfriend threw a punch at the dancer. His fist stopped mid-swing, blocked by a huge hand, Rush's hand. He had covered the span of the room in the time it took the boyfriend to wind up his punch. Rush twisted the wrist back with the kind of pressure that made the kid think his thumb was about to snap. With his other hand, Crush grabbed the ass-staring-dancer by the throat, hitting a particularly painful Kallaripayattu pressure point, and hauled the two kids out the side exit before most of the people on the dance floor even knew there was trouble. It was because of moments like this that the club owner paid Rush in cash and never bothered about things like withholding taxes or checking his past employment history.

Rush shoved them out into the night air. Ass Girl joined her boyfriend without missing a beat, asking him where they were going now. When Rush came back into the club, Gail was staring at him, like she was about to give him notes on his technique.

"Well?" Rush asked.

"Took too much effort."

"I'm not in the dojo."

"You're always in the dojo, Crush. When are you going to learn that?"

◎

Amelia had watched all this from the safety of a corner in the club with breathless amazement. The bouncer was everything she'd heard he was. He would do fine.

TWO

Back in the club, the underage girl was sipping her drink and wondering why there were chunks in it. The pretty studio exec was happily explaining to her wing girl the difference between a starter marriage and a bad first marriage. ("You know it's a failure going in!") The drunk at the east end of the bar was asking his shot glass what was wrong with his brain. And Amelia was watching Rush as he took his station again, standing by the bookshelf right next to her.

Amelia's clothes were casual, but stylish and clearly expensive. She'd found that balance between looking perfect and looking like she wasn't trying at all. This was what everybody aimed for and few people achieved. She was cool and easy, and that hungry look in her gray-green eyes only made her more desirable. Her hair was blond (this week) and hung carelessly upon her shoulders.

What those eyes did was scan the room. They looked the club over in much the same way Rush's eyes did, looking for something, just like he looked for trouble. But when they scanned to the left, her gaze kept landing on Rush's belt buckle, right there at eye level. Well, maybe not his belt buckle. But in that general vicinity. She'd look away and look back again, and every time her eyes would land on the bouncer's crotch, she'd smile a little broader, like she found the situation just plain funny. Pretty soon she was going to have to start laughing. He had a cell phone on his belt buckle, the old-fashioned flip kind. The phone on his belt buckle started blinking. She pretended to be laughing at that.

"Your crotch is blinking," she said.

"It happens," he said, not even looking down at her. His eyes were on the crowd. Three grab-ass jerks were trash-talking girls as they went into the ladies' room. Were they going to be trouble? Rush felt the scar on his head itch—his "Spidey sense" was trying to tell him something.

"Could be family," the girl said, still watching the blinking phone.

"Don't have a family."

"Poor orphan boy."

She snatched the phone from Rush's belt holster. He let her take it. She pressed "answer" and held it to her ear. A pretty ear.

"Hello."

"You're a girl!" said a young man on the other end of the line.

The young man was named Zerbe, and he was

Rush's brother. Sort of. Zerbe always called Rush just before midnight. That's when the walls started closing in on him. Usually Rush didn't answer, and Zerbe would leave him a rambling message. Sometimes Rush would pick up and tell his brother to leave him alone. But to have a girl answer? That made Zerbe's week. Hell, that made Zerbe's month.

"I know I'm female," she agreed. "What's the bouncer's name?"

"You don't want to know him," Zerbe said. "You want to know me. What's your name? What are you wearing? What's your favorite movie?"

"Don't get out much, do you?"

"I never get out. Lemme talk to my brother."

Rush was listening to Amelia's side of the conversation, but his eyes were on the underage girl with the underage boy. The girl was looking sleepy—her head kept lolling back, then jerking awake. The boy was talking a mile a minute.

"Here," Amelia said.

"I didn't answer it," Crush said.

"I did. He says he's your brother."

"That's his opinion," Rush said, grabbing the phone. "What's up?"

Zerbe didn't want to tell Rush about the walls closing in—that was old territory—so he just asked him what was going on there.

Rush read him the room, starting with the gangbangers. "C-Los and his tank are in back. Some assgrabbers by the ladies'. Maybe a rope master in the lounge." He looked down at Amelia and said, "a pick-pocket at the bar."

"Not the work shit, the fun shit. Remember fun, Caleb?" Zerbe was the only one who called Rush by his first name—he'd earned the right—and even he only did so on rare occasions. "Tell me about the girl. Her voice sounds blond—is she blond?"

Rush looked around for the underage girl and her pursuer. They were gone. He tossed the phone back to Amelia.

"You talk to him," he told her, then moved off to where the young couple had been sitting. A busgirl was clearing their spot. He stopped her and checked out the girl's glass. A swirl of bluish backwash remained in the bottom. He hurried out the door, vaulting over the red-velvet rope that kept the hopefuls at bay, and ran into the parking lot.

Back inside, Amelia took a picture of herself with Rush's phone and sent it to Zerbe. He was right. She was blond. In her early twenties, with the kind of hair that made him want to bury his face in it and the kind of green eyes that he wanted to look at him in the morning without a tinge of regret in them.

Zerbe asked her to marry him. He was joking, but he wouldn't have turned her down if she said yes.

She laughed. It was a nice laugh. "Why don't you come down here?"

"Can't," he said. "Did you ever see one of those

movies where they keep a brain alive in a jar?"

"No."

"I'm a brain alive in a jar."

Zerbe scratched at the spot he could never quite reach under the electronic tether on his ankle and asked her again if she'd marry him.

"No," she said, as nicely as you can say that. "Have your brother call me."

"He won't."

"Sure, he will," she said. "I've got his phone."

And the line went dead.

◎

Los Angeles shuts down early. People think it's a wild town, Sodom and Gomorrah on the Pacific, but it closes up almost as early as Salt Lake City. By one in the morning, most everything's quiet, and the streets are deserted. The Nocturne was open later than most nightspots, but everything around it was dark and shuttered, so it was easy for the black Lamborghini Murciélago to keep cruising the nearby streets, like a stealth bomber on a night mission. Now and again, the driver's window would roll down and a forearm like a side of beef would slide out as the driver surveyed the parking lot. The ink work on his shoulder was spectacular: a skeleton in a vat of acid, reaching up at two angels flying above him, straining to grab God's messengers and drag them to a boiling death.

Misery loves company.

◎

The parking lot behind the Nocturne has a history. Jean Harlow had a fight with her second husband there the night before he killed himself. There's no plaque or anything to mark the spot. This city just doesn't respect its heritage.

Seventy-five years later, the underage boy was loading the underage girl into the back of his Scion. She was snoring and limp as a rag doll. The grab-ass jerks were with him. One of them reached out and grabbed the girl's tit.

The boy slapped his hand away. "Hey! I go first. I'm her date."

Now there was another hand in the mix. A man's hand, tapping the underage boy on the shoulder. The kid twisted around, annoyed. A big guy in a black T-shirt was butting in.

"My girlfriend's wasted and I'm taking her home," the kid said. "You got a problem with that?"

Rush smiled. "Just so you know, the manufacturer of the drug Rohypnol—you call it a roofie—has recently reformulated the pill to make it turn bright blue in most beverages. Yet another example of your pharmaceutical companies looking after you, the consumer."

"Is this your fucking business?"

The boy laughed with his friends and started to say

something about Rush thinking he was all that, but before he could finish, Rush had the kid's palm bent back against his wrist and he was on his knees, crying in pain.

The two grab-asses came at Rush. He blocked the first guy's punch and dropkicked the second one behind the ear, yanking him off balance with the crook of his ankle and sending him to the asphalt.

Amelia was watching the whole thing from the corner of the building, all lit up and enjoying herself, like this was WWF on cable.

The second grab-ass was still on the pavement—he wasn't unconscious or anything, he just seemed to think that lying still was the best way to deal with the situation. The other one was staring at Rush like he wasn't sure what was going on but he'd gotten the message that moving was a bad idea.

Rush spoke calmly to the underage boy, "Okay, I'm going to let go."

He let go. The kid took a swing at him. Rush grabbed the wrist again, but this time when he bent it, he didn't stop. The joint snapped like a gunshot. The kid screamed.

Rush locked eyes with grab-ass number one.

"Your choice," he said.

Grab-ass took one deep breath. Then he ran off. His pal scrambled to his feet and joined him, leaving their mastermind to cry and cradle his broken wrist. Rush sighed and stepped over him. He slung the unconscious girl over his shoulder and headed back toward the club.

Amelia was watching all this like she'd just found out that Santa was real. There was a little crowd with her now—party girls catcalling and cheering on the home team. She turned to one of them and asked what the bouncer's name was.

"Girl, you do not want to mess with that one," was the answer.

"Just tell me his name," Amelia said.

A tattooed Latina piped up. "Crush. He was in some kind of Mexican prison gang."

A Valley girl smacked her down. "He's not Mexican, stupid! He's Bulgarian or something."

"Nobody's Bulgarian." This from an Asian-Anglo Brentwood-looking girl.

"Well, he speaks Bulgarian or something," Valley Girl maintained.

An Armenian brunette from Glendale was sure she knew it all. "No, he's Italian! I heard his dad was all connected and Crush got in trouble for doing some wise guy's wife!"

The Latina hated this chick. "You don't know nothing, bitch. He—"

The girls scattered like geese when they saw Rush approaching them, the snoring girl drooped over his shoulder like a sack of sand. They all scattered except for one.

"Impressive," Amelia said as Rush strolled by.

"That's why I did it, to impress you," he said, without breaking his stride.

He rounded the corner toward the club entrance, with its red-velvet rope and line of hopefuls waiting to get in. The cool and the not cool enough. The Lamborghini came out of nowhere.

Fishtailing through the crowd and screeching to a halt, it stopped just shy of smashing into the side of the building and crushing Amelia between its carbon-fiber body and the building's hard red brick. Somehow, the bystanders managed to dive out of the way without getting hit. The gull-wing door of the Lamborghini flew up and pinned Amelia to the wall, the way a bored cat traps a moth against a window.

The driver, sporting a large skeleton tattoo, looked at her. Not angry, just doing his job. A professional.

"Gotcha," he said, as he started to climb out of the car to get her.

THREE

The thing about fancy-ass sports cars is that they're made to drive, not to get in and out of. A big guy like Skeleton Tattoo had to swivel around and hoist himself out, and that gave Amelia time to shove down on the door and slide to the asphalt. Before Skeleton Tat could kick the door open again, she'd skittered under the car and come up out the other side.

The passenger-side gull-wing door flew up, and a different hand reached out and grabbed her ankle. This hand had big blue veins and some nasty rings tattooed on each finger, and when Amelia kicked back and drove the heel of her fuck-me pumps into the knuckles, it didn't seem to mind one bit.

Rush was still holding the unconscious girl over his shoulder. The people around him were getting up from the pavement where they'd dived to avoid the Lamborghini, checking to see if they had any broken bones and wondering what the hell was going on. Rush had one big advantage in situations like this—he didn't spend a lot of time wondering why things were happening. Gail called it "reacting to command." When something happened, he didn't think, he just moved.

He slung the sleeping girl off his shoulder and handed her to some startled club goers, like he was passing them the ketchup at a cookout. They grabbed the girl because the big man told them to and watched as Rush seized Amelia by the wrists and pulled her away from the car. The hand with the tattooed rings wouldn't let go, but that was fine with Rush. He used Amelia to drag the man out of the car.

When Rings tumbled onto the pavement, Rush stomped on his arm. This made him let go of Amelia, who crawled away, her tight skirt tearing as her knees scraped the asphalt. Skeleton Tat was out now, moving around the car with confident ease, investigating this little complication. Rush hit him with a roundhouse kick to the head. This wasn't the helpful ankle-pull to the back of the neck he'd given the ass-grabber; it was a full-strength punch to the temple, using the ball of his foot as a fist. Skeleton Tat went down like he'd been hit by a hammer.

Rings leapt up, pouncing onto Rush's back. Rush swung around and they both fell across the hood of the car.

Amelia was struggling to get to her feet. One guy in the crowd stepped forward to help pull her up. It was a nice thing to do. Skeleton Tat was up now. He grabbed Amelia by the hair. The nice guy was considering playing the hero when Skeleton Tat pulled a pistol from the back of his pants. That made the nice guy run. Guns are good for that.

Rings had Rush down on the hood of the Lamborghini and was trying to choke him. The scar on Rush's bald head was blazing red, but even with Rings's big hands, he couldn't really damage that thick neck. So Rings pressed the point of his elbow down on Rush's Adam's apple, trying to crush his windpipe. Muscles can't protect that spot, no matter how strong they are. Rush reached up over his head, fingers scrambling for a weapon. He found the windshield wiper. He yanked forward, snapping it off and lashing Rings across the face. Rings reared back, a bloody welt on his cheek.

Skeleton Tat shoved Amelia into the passenger seat of the Lamborghini. Rush rolled back up onto the windshield and kicked out with his legs, slamming the gull-wing door down on Skeleton Tat's back. Jumping to his feet, he shoved the door again, crashing it down on Tat's head. Rings came at him from behind—Rush gave him a back kick to the face, using his counterweight to press down on the door.

Skeleton Tat roared and reared back, shoving the door open with his shoulders, flinging Rush away. Tat spun around, pistol in his hand, ready to end this annoyance once and for all. Rush kept his balance and shifted his weight to move inside the arc of Tat's swinging arm—he grabbed the gunman's wrist and kept spinning, wheeling him around. Digging his fingers into the man's tendons, Rush forced him to loosen his grip on the gun. Wrenching it from Tat's hand, he popped out the cartridge, kicking it away into the street.

Amelia was leaning out of the car now, watching. "Cool," she said.

But Rings was on her now, a large hunting knife pressed to her throat. He was bleeding and angry, and he really wanted this to be over.

"Gedbagin," he said, in an accent so heavy she could hardly understand him. He pressed the blade into her flesh and shoved toward the gull-wing door—she understood him then. He wanted her to get back in the car.

Before she could do it, she was startled by an unfamiliar voice yelling at them in thick, Slavic-sounding gibberish. She appeared surprised to see that Rush was doing the shouting. Rings answered with some gibberish of his own, and then pushed Amelia the rest of the way into the car. She fell across the driver's seat, knocking over a pile of CDs, scattering rainbows everywhere.

Rush hurried around to the car door, but Skeleton Tat was in front of him again. It had taken Tat a while to realize that Rush was a serious threat, but now he knew it and he was on his game. Crouching low, he punched Rush in the gut with a sledgehammer fist. Rush went down. Tat kicked him before he could hit the pavement, then kicked him again. And again. Rush grabbed the fender of the car and braced himself against the kicks, taking the pain, ready to do something with it.

The car started. Engine roaring, the Lamborghini lurched forward. Rush lost his hold and hit the asphalt. Tat looked startled, like he couldn't believe Rings was leaving without him.

The distraction was what Rush had been waiting for. He pivoted his legs around and smashed his heel into Tat's knee with an ugly crunch.

Rings threw the car into reverse and tried to back over Rush, but he had already rolled to the side. He leapt up and reached in the car window, grabbing the shoulder harness and wrapping it around Rings's throat, choking him.

"Turn off the engine," Rush told him.

Rings didn't move. It was a standoff.

Amelia saw her moment. From her vantage point in the passenger seat, she looked around wildly for a weapon. Her hands scrambled at the loose pile of CDs in the back, two acrylic fingernails popping off like tiddlywinks. She snatched up one of the silvery discs and bent it against the dashboard, snapping it in half, then swung it around and pressed the jagged edge against Rings's bulging throat.

"Do it!" she said.

Rush just had time to admire her quick thinking and notice the fear in Rings's eyes—not out of recognition that Amelia could really hurt him, but from the knowledge that he was surrounded by lunatics who didn't know how to behave when reasonably threatened. Then Amelia flung up the car door and jumped out.

She could have warned him, Rush thought.

Rings hit the gas, safety harness strangling him or no, and the Lamborghini shot backward. Hanging on with his big arms, his feet flying, Rush felt the car pivot out into the street. He let go as Rings shifted gears. Hitting the pavement with a vicious thud, he rolled, feeling his skin burn and tear. The sports car squealed away into the night.

Rush lay on the asphalt, looking up at the tan-gray sky that passes for night in L.A. He thought, *This is going to hurt in the morning.* Then he laughed as he realized how much it hurt right now. He pulled himself to his feet, peeling a shredded piece of T-shirt from the pavement burn on his shoulder and silently cataloging his other injuries. He tried to use his Zen meditation training to stop them from hurting. It didn't work.

The spectators were still there—farther back, but watching the show. The party girls were going to have more Crush stories to share. One girl was missing, though. The one with the blond hair and the hungry eyes, the object of this whole mess. Rush smiled and noticed to his surprise that he still had all his teeth—even the fake ones. The underage boy was gone too—he must have used the distraction to take his broken arm home. Rush wondered what story he'd cook up for his parents. He'd probably try one on the underage girl too, when she woke up. She looked dim enough to believe him.

Gail made her way through the crowd toward him. Great. Now he'd get a review of his performance. Maybe he should have stayed on the Lamborghini.

"He got away," she said.

Rush wasn't sure who she meant at first—then he realized that Skeleton Tattoo was missing as well. That made it a clean sweep. But at least they hadn't gotten that girl. Whoever the fuck she was.

Before Gail had a chance to say more, Rush spotted something on the pavement. Maybe a shiny distraction would delay the inevitable critique. He picked it up—it was the busted half of the CD. The girl must have dropped it when she made her retreat. He read what was left of the label.

"I wouldn't have pegged them for Adele fans," he said.

Gail laughed. The critique could wait until their next lesson. For now, she had to take care of his wounds. He tossed the CD shard and walked with her back into the club.

FOUR

Gail had tended to a wounded Rush before. A couple of years ago, he'd taken a gig protecting a popular female singer from the paparazzi in general and from her ex-husband in particular. The cause of the tug-of-war was the couple's four-year-old daughter. Each claimed the other was an unfit parent. Each was probably right.

The continued stress of the legal battles led the twenty-two-year-old mother and the twenty-four-year-old father to endless nights of clubbing and drinking and drugging, followed by weeks in rehab, followed by more clubbing and drinking and drugging. In the meantime, the daughter spent most of her time with Rush—he felt more like a nanny than a bodyguard. Still, she was a good kid, and she showed a remarkable aptitude for Muay Thai, or at least the kid-friendly version of Thai boxing that Rush practiced with her when playing with Barbie lost its charm.

He was picking the girl up from a play date while

her mom was sleeping off one of her own, when they jumped him. Rush wasn't sure how they knew the girl's schedule—maybe the singer's mom, who, you guessed it, was estranged from her daughter, told the ex-husband, thinking she'd get to see her granddaughter more if he got sole custody. At any rate, the plan was simple: hire some goons to kidnap the girl, thereby showing that the singer couldn't protect the kid. Maybe the ex-hubby was planning on staging a daring rescue to cement his own cause. He was enough of an idiot to think that would work.

The plan never got that far.

Rush ended up with various cuts and bruises and welts. The would-be kidnappers ended up with seven broken bones between them. The little girl ended up in her crying mother's arms—once Mom had come to. (Mother and daughter moved to New York to get away from it all, and Rush lost the job. Last he heard, the singer and her ex were back together, for the sake of the kid. God help her.)

Rush had come home to his loft in downtown L.A. after the attempted kidnapping, stiff and sore. Gail dropped by later on, with a bottle of healing oil. Rush stripped down and she went to work on him, kneading his tight muscles, digging her elbow into his stiff joints, spreading the warm oil all over his flesh, never having to ask where the hurt was, the two of them communicating on some sort of nonverbal, purely physical level.

From the sofa, Zerbe had watched this the way

he watched everything—for the vicarious thrill. K. C. Zerbe was Rush's younger half-brother—well, actually not his brother at all. Rush's mother had been the third trophy wife of Zerbe's father. That made them not related by blood. In Rush's opinion, that was the best kind of relation you could have.

It struck Zerbe as odd, as he had watched Gail rub every inch of Rush's body, that there wasn't a damn thing sexual about it for either of them. It was just physical therapy. Zerbe was sure he'd have had a happy ending before she stopped drizzling the oil on him. But then, Zerbe didn't get out much, as he was the first to admit.

While that, or something very much like it, was going on in a back room at the Nocturne after Rush's run-in with Tat and Rings, Zerbe was just playing with the picture Amelia had sent him on his cell phone. Since she hadn't told him her name, he hacked into the LAPD face-recognition program to see if she had a record. Despite what you see on TV, hacking into a secure server takes time and effort, but Zerbe had so much of the former that the latter went without saying. While the faces flashed by on the screen, trying to make a match with hers, he decided to reward himself by going into the kitchenette and making a peanut butter and banana sandwich. Who said he didn't lead a rich, full life?

They were out of bananas. By that time of night, Rush would be heading home. Zerbe figured he'd call and ask him to pick some up on the way. He'd do the same for Rush, if he could. He'd pressed Rush's auto-dial on his cell phone before he remembered who he was calling.

"Hello." It was Amelia. Zerbe had forgotten that she still had Rush's phone.

"Ah," Zerbe said. "I was calling my brother."

"Just a sec."

Zerbe was puzzled. He heard her say, "It's for you."

"Hello," Rush said, the phone having been passed. "Can't talk right now, Zerbe. A girl's got a gun to the back of my head."

That never happens to me, Zerbe thought.

⊚

Rush had left the club a little after one, strolling across the darkened parking lot toward his red 1966 Pontiac GTO convertible. John DeLorean's contribution to American culture. The ultimate muscle car.

He rolled his sore shoulder under the fresh T-shirt, thanked the Lord (whoever He was) that Gail was in his life, and remembered to scan the perimeter, making sure the Lamborghini was nowhere in sight. What he didn't notice was the tiny scratch on the GTO's passenger-side window frame, which would have told him that someone had taken a coat hanger to the door. Nobody's perfect.

He was on the 101 when his cell phone rang. He

reached down to his belt clip to answer it. It was empty. That's right, he had left the phone with—

"I got it," said a voice coming from the back seat. He turned his head and was greeted with the barrel of a Beretta. Amelia was nestled back there, gun in one hand, cell phone in the other.

She answered the phone and then handed it to Rush, who told Zerbe that he couldn't talk right now on account of the gun to his head.

He pressed a button to end the call, flipped the phone shut, and tossed it into the passenger seat.

"That's one old-ass phone," Amelia said.

"It works. That's all I ask from a phone."

"It doesn't have any numbers memorized, or Facebook or anything. Don't you have any friends?"

"No, I'm an asshole."

She frowned and shifted the gun to the other hand, bored, like it was a toy. "This is a big-ass car."

"It's to compensate for my freakishly small dick. You know, that gun would have come in handy back at the club."

"Yeah, I forgot it in my car."

"Oh, so you have a car, too. Can I ask why you decided to hitch a ride with me?"

"They might know what my car looks like. They might follow me."

"Who are they?"

"Them."

"You knew this was my car?"

"I asked around. You've got quite a fan base at the club."

"I don't let it go to my head."

"I want to hire you to be my bodyguard."

Rush pressed his foot on the accelerator. He weaved between the neighboring cars as the GTO ate up the road. "Well, I usually get work through referrals, but this is nice, this makes a change."

The GTO was tearing along the freeway like a rocket.

"I'm Stanley Trask's daughter," Amelia said.

Rush's face took on a stern expression. "My fee just doubled."

The city lights were flying by. Amelia was getting scared. "Slow down."

"No. This way, if you shoot me, you end up looking like one of those high school driver's-ed movies. Ain't no airbags in this baby."

He reached with his hand to the back seat, palm open. She dropped the gun into it and sat back, sulking. "You're no fun." But the car kept speeding along the 101. "So slow down!"

"We're being followed."

She turned to look out the back window—the Lamborghini was a few car lengths behind them, bearing down. It was a duel between Italian and American engineering. Amelia was interested to see how it would turn out.

FIVE

To understand about Stanley Trask, you have to go back a few years to when things were simpler. To the time when Rush had a steady job and Zerbe was in prison. The good old days.

Tigon Security was run by Victoria Donleavy, an ex-cop with short-cropped gray hair that was almost the same color as her gray suit. She wore her blouse buttoned all the way up, no makeup, and flat orthopedic shoes, all in an attempt to tone down her earthy sexiness, which still flared up sometimes, especially when she got angry, which was fairly often. Her years with LAPD had taught her that women, if they were going to be taken seriously, had better not be attractive, threatening, or female. This dead-end had led her to an early retirement and a desire to beat law enforcement at its own game. Tigon was one of the best, most profitable private security companies on the west coast.

For her team, Donleavy recruited only the finest graduates of the military, the penal system, and the

L.A. street gangs. With Rush, she had a trifecta. Tigon's clients were the rich and the famous; if you had to ask how much they charged, you couldn't even afford a referral.

Stanley Trask didn't have to ask. He and his brother Walter ran GlobalInterLink, the Biggest Communications Company in the World. Their words, but true nonetheless. Cell phones, computers, e-readers, satellite TVs—it was well on its way to actually being the biggest company in the world.

Success breeds enemies. The Trasks had been receiving threatening letters, letters that Tigon Security (and Rush) had deemed credible. The Tigon Threat Assessment Team had made this claim after examining the letters using a variety of psychological and criminological criteria. Rush had made this claim after meeting Stanley Trask and deciding that he was a filthy rich, arrogant asshole who a whole lot of people probably wanted dead. The more Rush got to know Trask, the more sure he was that this initial assessment had been correct. Trask stole software from his competitors, stole money from his stockholders, and probably stole loose change from his left pocket when his right pocket wasn't looking. In other words, it was an honor to be protecting the guy.

But protecting him Rush was. Rush was a part of the Tigon team, and theirs was not to wonder why, theirs was but to shut up and follow orders. That was how, three years ago, he'd found himself in a van outside the Marina, putting lotion on his nose, preparing for a shift in the blazing sun on the deck of Trask's yacht. He looked at his partner, Tony Guzman, ensconced comfortably behind monitors, earphones in place and Dr. Pepper in hand, and felt a twinge of resentment. The van was equipped with video, supplying views of the yacht, inside and out, as well as audio surveillance. It also had air conditioning and its own bathroom. It didn't seem fair.

"How come you get to sit in here and play with yourself and I have to go stand in the hot sun?" Rush asked.

Guzman was Rush's best friend, but all is fair in love and getting out of shithole assignments. "It's surrounded by water. I can't swim. If I could swim, I'd be there for you, Crush."

The rear door to the van opened with a rush of sunlight, street noise, and hot air. Donleavy blotted all that out with her anger. "Crush, goddammit, don't talk. The Principal does not want to hear your voice."

"The Principal" was how they referred to the one being protected, which in this case meant Stanley Trask. Trask had been present during a discussion of whether or not terrorists might be responsible for the ongoing death threats, when Rush had offered the opinion that the perp just might be one of the couple of hundred people who hated Trask's guts. The conversation had lagged after that, Rush remembered.

Rush nodded, obediently. Donleavy looked at the

monitor—the operative on duty was shifting from foot to foot on the yacht's deck.

"And somebody take over for Stegner before he wets himself," Donleavy said, as she left to go make nice to The Principal.

When she was gone, Guzman bet Rush five bucks that Stegner could hold out for another ten minutes. Rush won.

The thing about surveillance duty, Rush reflected, is that you just have to stand there. That's it. You can't let your mind wander, not if you're any good. You can't be thinking about what or who you're going to do that night, because at any moment the boredom might be shattered by an odd creak of the floorboard, and if your fantasy life is too rich, well, you might miss it and go in later to find your Principal with his throat cut. This is what's called a rookie mistake.

So the thing you do is, you just stand there. Looking imposing, immovable. Scanning the area with your eyes. Keeping your ears open for unusual sounds. Even your nose is sensitive for gas or perfume. And ninety-nine-point-nine times out of a hundred, nothing, absolutely nothing out of the ordinary, happens. Still, you stand there. Because that's what you're paid to do.

Rush didn't shift from one foot to another. He kept his weight equally balanced between them. Ready to go either way. To the right was Stanley Trask's cabin. To the left was Walter Trask's cabin. Rush didn't have to look inside to know that Walter's would be the smaller of the two. Walter was Stanley's twin brother—the younger by twenty minutes, Stanley always said. Always. Walter had the same fish face that Stanley had, but somehow on Walter it looked weak, whereas on Stanley it looked like it was about to swallow you whole. Walter did most of the real work in GlobalInterLink, Rush was sure, while Stanley took the glory. Walter always sucked hind tit. Stanley got the glorious boobs.

Rush had been standing on that yacht for two hours, doing nothing and doing a damn fine job of it, when a lovely young woman in a dark business suit strolled down the gangway. Rush stepped to block her way.

"I'm here to see Stanley Trask," she said in a lilting Slavic accent. Upon closer inspection, her business suit looked like it would come off her lithe, sleek body at the slightest encouragement.

"And what is it regarding?" Rush asked, in his deepest, most imposing voice.

"Oral, I think," she answered. "Unless he wants to pay extra."

Sometimes you just have to talk to The Principal. Rush went below deck and knocked on his cabin door. Stanley Trask opened it. His ruddy face seemed to extrude from his bulging bathrobe.

"Mr. Trask, there's a woman here to see you," Rush said. "She says her name is Tianna. With two Ns."

Trask beamed. "Send her in!"

"Mr. Trask, you hired us to protect you. There is no

way we can do a background check on this woman on such short notice."

Trask wiped his hands with antibacterial gel (coconut-lime-verbena-scented, he could tell) and spoke to Rush like a patient uncle. "Listen. The people who sent me those death threats, do you know what they're trying to do? They're trying to affect me, trying to change my way of life. Change my path, as it were. Now I could listen to them—I could run scared. Or I could choose to defy them. Well, I choose defiance. I stick to my path."

There you had it—if that hooker didn't give Stanley Trask a blowjob right now, the terrorists would have won. It was so patriotic it made Rush want to puke.

So he went back on deck to get Tianna. Guzman had volunteered to leave the homey confines of the surveillance van to relieve Rush while he went down to visit Trask. When Rush re-joined them, she was handing Guzman a business card.

"Nice embossing," Guzman said to Rush, a little embarrassed.

Nice embossing indeed.

But that meant that there was a period of about three minutes when only Stegner was in the van, watching the monitors. In the postmortem, after all the damage was done, Stegner swore he never fell asleep at his post, nor did he take his eyes off the monitors to empty his bladder. So just how did Bob Steinkellner get on the boat? Magic, Rush decided. Pure and simple magic.

Bob Steinkellner was a magician, after all. He specialized in that most difficult and unappreciated form of prestidigitation, sleight of hand. Coin tricks, to be precise. So transporting his three-hundred-pound body from dock to yacht without being seen was not exactly in his wheelhouse.

Bob started doing magic when he was small, like a lot of boys do. They think that if they learn the card and coin and matchbox tricks from *The Blackstone Book of Magic and Illusions*, they'll be more popular and get invited to more parties and, let's face it, get girls. The fact that performing magic actively repels members of the opposite sex is something that never occurs to them until it's too late. By then, the damage is done. They're hooked. Poof! They're magicians.

At least that's the way it seemed to Bob Steinkellner, once his early middle age had set in and he saw what magic had done to his life. Poof! It had disappeared! It had disappeared in the hours, weeks, months spent locked in his room, perfecting finger rolls and the Dancing Handkerchief illusion. Disappeared in the ten years spent performing at children's birthday parties and old folks' homes and, disastrously, at a few bachelor parties. Disappeared in endless afternoons at the Magic Castle, the magician's club, talking with other (what he now called) magic-holics about how David Copperfield was a hack and David Blaine was a poser and Ricky Jay was the only halfway decent sleight-of-hand artist around, but when *they* hit the big time, they'd show the world what magic could really be.

Then, when he hit thirty-four, it happened. He realized that he fucking hated doing magic tricks. Loathed them. Despised them. Every time he cracked open a new deck to do the Amazing Card through the Window Trick, one that had taken him months to perfect and that he used to perform with relish, he felt his skin crawl. Every time he demonstrated the Magnetic Match Trick, he could barely stop from retching. Every time he did the Coin Optical Illusion, he felt himself die a little inside.

Was this all there was?

The Amazing Life Disappearing Trick. Abracadabra.

He considered forming a group, Magicians Anonymous, to help others who shared his affliction. "My name's Bob," he would declare to the gathered sufferers, "and I'm a magician." But he couldn't get anyone to join. He couldn't even get anyone to see what a soul-devouring addiction magic was. Everyone he knew was a magician, and they seemed to like, if not love, that life-wasting disease. They told him to take some time off. With a little break, they told him, he'd get back in touch with what he loved about magic.

That was the last thing Bob wanted.

So, like an alcoholic whose friends are all drinkers, Bob found himself alone. What's more, the bitter irony of his situation was that magic was his only vocation. The only trade he knew. And he made if not a good living at it, at least a living. It paid the rent. It put food on his table. If he saved up enough, he could even take a girl out once or twice a month. If he ever met one.

So that was Bob Steinkellner's dilemma: He'd become the magician who hated magic. He cursed under his breath every time he put on his black tights and got ready to perform the Escape from the Straight Jacket Trick. How could he escape from this?

That's when Stanley Trask came into his life.

Bob's Aha Moment came, oddly enough, when he read about Trask's Aha Moment in an old issue of *O Magazine*, while waiting in a dentists' office for an appointment he could ill afford. The Aha Moment—the column in which wildly successful, incredibly self-important people talk about the point in their lives whern their path diverged from the ordinary (read, your path) and ascended to the extraordinary (read: Oprah's path). Stanley Trask's Aha Moment was refreshingly free of humility and self-deprecation. He just related the time he realized that people wanted to be in touch with each other all the time. It was 1986, and Stanley was on the Amtrak from Washington to New York—he was already rich, he confessed, but not superrich. He noticed someone three rows ahead pulling out one of those Motorola brick phones from his briefcase and placing a call—or rather, trying to place a call, since, from the way he was shouting into the mouthpiece, he wasn't getting much reception. "Can you hear me now?" he was asking. "Can you hear me?" From tiny acorns, mighty oaks grow.

Now, Trask was not an inventor. Or an idea man. What he did was invest in other people's new technologies and leverage them in such a way that the potential positive or negative outcomes were enhanced. In other words (and not the words he used in his Aha Moment), Stanley Trask was a thief.

He got in on the ground floor when the first GSM network opened in Finland and rode the 2G-phone wave as it literally took over the world. Mobile phones went from bulky car phones to sleek handheld devices. Suddenly, they were necessities—people were incomplete without them. Stanley Trask (and a few others) ruled the world.

Bob Steinkellner wanted in.

He got all his money, and his mother's money, and even some of his dad's money together and opened his very own branch of the Stanley Trask empire in South Pasadena. After much research, consisting (he was to discover afterward) of reading mostly self-serving puff pieces written by Trask's employees and posted on various websites beholding to Trask, he took the plunge and purchased a franchise outlet, selling the newest of Trask's contributions to twenty-first-century telecommunications. Just off the 110 on Fair Oaks Avenue, Steinkellner's store wasn't much, but it was a start. He was one of the lucky few (he was told) to get in on the ground floor of Feniro Wireless, the new brand from GlobalInterLink. A combination wireless phone and

GPS satellite system, it would allow family members to stay in touch with one another, let parents track their children's whereabouts, and enable them to set spending limits on texting and downloadable content. It would be a boon to worried mothers and fathers.

Unfortunately, it was the single un-coolest phone in the short history of mobile communications. To America's youth, it screamed, "I'm on an electronic leash, and my parents won't let me off it."

It lasted eighteen months on the market.

Seventeen months into the phone's life, Bob sat alone in his distressingly empty store when the phone rang. Hope used to spring in his chest every time the phone rang—would it be a potential customer asking for directions to the store? Someone calling to reserve a phone? Now, he knew it would be a wrong number or a prank call. They were all he ever got.

"Bob Steinkellner? Stanley Trask here."

And it was. Bob knew that voice from innumerable appearances on Larry King and that one time when he was a guest fire-er on *Celebrity Apprentice*. Bob's heart leapt to his throat—the Great Man was actually calling him.

"I need your help, Bob. And you need mine."

All he was asking for was a show of faith. If Bob would order as many phones as possible to help the company through the next fiscal year, then they would prosper together. "You have two choices, Bob," Stanley (for they were on a first-name basis now) said. "You can either help this company we've built together, or you can help destroy it."

Bob looked around the store at the walls full of cell phones, many of which had sat there for months. Could he afford to double that inventory? No, he could not.

"I'll do it," Bob said. How could he say anything else to Stanley Trask?

So he ordered the phones, doubling his inventory; he showed the world that he still had faith in Feniro.

One month later, the company went bankrupt.

The press termed the telephone calls that Stanley Trask placed to all his distributors "channel stuffing." This is a practice in which the seller forces as much product possible into its distribution channels. Coca-Cola has done it. Sunbeam has done it. Even Chrysler did it. It wasn't strictly illegal. Not strictly. It was a simple strategy for survival—better someone else gets stuck with inventory than you.

The Feniro bankruptcy was the first failure of Stanley Trask's career. He took it philosophically. "It was a bad idea, badly executed and badly marketed. To be honest, I took my eye off the ball. But I've learned from my mistakes. I assure you, it won't happen again."

And he went on to mounting success.

Bob Steinkellner? Not so much. He lost the store—but not the phones. He was forced to go back to live with his mother. And worse than that, far worse, he had to return to magic. But in the new economy—when parents stopped throwing lavish birthday parties for their kids, when companies stopped hiring entertainment for their corporate retreats, when the competition for gigs grew greater and greater—there just wasn't much room for a self-hating magician.

So with his money running out, with his mother weeping in the next room, Bob Steinkellner watched a news report on Stanley Trask and his growing empire. Feniro Wireless was mentioned in passing, humorously, as his one misstep.

Bob Steinkellner decided, then and there, that he had to make a statement.

He went to the library to go on the internet (his home connection was cut off due to lack of payment) and did his research. He learned how to make a pipe bomb from watching videos on YouTube. He found out about Trask's yacht from TMZ. He located it on Google Earth and got directions to it from MapQuest. All in an afternoon.

From his mom's Ford Taurus, he waited and watched at the marina while Trask came and went, day after day. Trask was living there while divorcing his third wife, a budding TV star. The divorce got more press than Feniro's bankruptcy ever had. Security was tight, and the guards were awesomely proportioned. He nearly gave up, nearly decided to kill himself, nearly decided to give magic another go, when he saw his chance.

The gangplank (or whatever they called it) was empty. No massive guard stood at attention. Before he knew what he was doing, Bob Steinkellner jumped out of his car, ran across the dock, and slipped on board. Presto!

Rush had gone back to his station after the discussion with Stanley and Tianna. He'd stood there for about twenty minutes when all hell broke loose. A crash from below decks. And a high-pitched scream. Rush was down there in a second, flinging open the door.

Trask was holding Tianna down and slapping her. Tianna was crying. Trask was naked and red as a lobster with rage.

Rush stepped inside the cabin and locked the door behind him. In a situation like this, a bodyguard has to use his best judgment to decide if this is a role-playing game or the real thing. Tianna's tears and bloody lip told him all he needed to know.

He reached down and plucked the naked Trask off her like a bear off a salmon. Trask's limp dick told him this hadn't been about sex.

"She was looking through my papers!" Trask shouted, enraged.

"I wasn't!" Tianna said, weeping. Rush saw now that she was naked, too. Lithe and lean like a cheetah. Not instinctively covering herself—nudity was clearly not an unusual state for her. "I was looking for a condom. I forgot mine."

"I was just paying for a blowjob," Trask said.

"You expect me to suck that bareback?" she said, with disdain.

Trask went for her again. Rush held him back.

Rush heard a rapping at the door, followed by Guzman calling, "Mr. Trask?"

Trask was bending over to pick up his pants and pull his wallet out. Rush saw more of him than he would have liked.

"There's a merger coming up. If it leaks, I'll lose billions," Trask explained. He offered Rush a fistful of hundred-dollar bills and glanced at the girl. "Make this go away. I don't care how."

Rush looked at the money.

Donleavy had joined Guzman outside. "Mr. Trask, is everything all right?"

Rush still looked at the money. "Is that how much you paid *her*?"

Trask grinned with his bonded teeth. "It's what I was *going* to pay her. I'm giving it to you now. For services rendered."

Outside the cabin, Donleavy and Guzman were startled to hear the sounds of struggle, punctuated by low-pitched grunts and spitting noises. Guzman threw his big frame against the bulkhead, once, twice.

The door flew off its hinges. The first sight that greeted them was Tianna standing buck-naked and with her jaw hanging open. The second sight was the one that put that astonished look on her face.

Rush was sitting on a naked Trask and shoving hundred-dollar bills in his mouth, one at time.

But as he said to Donleavy when they pulled him off Trask, at least he wasn't *talking* to The Principal.

Didn't that count for anything?

"You're fired," Donleavy said. Given the circumstances, Rush couldn't blame her.

Guzman and Stegner were escorting Rush and Tianna off the boat, to the sound of Donleavy's effusive apologies to Trask, when Rush saw it. A pipe bomb taped to the railing of the hallway outside Trask's cabin. He thought about moving on without saying a word, but he had Guzman and Donleavy to think about. And even Stegner. The guy was a total douchebag, but Rush didn't really want to see him with metal shrapnel studding his face.

They didn't believe him at first, at least Stegner didn't. He thought Rush was joking or playing for time or trying to get his job back. Then Guzman went back to have a look.

They evacuated the yacht just in time. The last of the kitchen crew was crossing the gangplank when the bomb went off. A loud pop and billow of drifting smoke. What the hell, Rush thought. It looked like a something out of a magic act. Something to, what was the phrase, divert the eye? At that moment, someone stepped on deck from below. Two someones. One close behind the other, holding an arm around his neck. As the smoke cleared, Rush could just make out his fish-like features. In the mad rush to evacuate the boat, one man had been forgotten: Walter Trask, the always neglected younger brother. Wouldn't you know it?

There was a huge hunting knife held tight to his

neck, and the man behind him kept leading him forward until they were clear of the smoke and in full view. Then the man stopped, cleared his throat, and positioned Walter Trask a little to the side, so that he could take the stage.

"I want television cameras here!" the man declared. "I want to make a statement. I have Stanley Trask, and I'm prepared to kill him."

"Fuck you!" Stanley Trask roared from beside Rush on the dock. He had a bathrobe on now, but it was hanging open in front, and Trask didn't mind one bit. "You don't have me, you fat fag!"

The man looked troubled. Then he took a good look at his hostage. Despite being identical twins, Walter and Stanley weren't hard to tell apart. For one thing, Walter didn't shave his head—he kept a monkish ring of gray hair around the crown of his skull. For another, Walter didn't live the life of a rock star as much as his brother did, and consequentially, his face had a more relaxed, healthier glow about it. It also sagged a bit more, since it hadn't been artificially lifted and Botoxed. In short, Walter looked like a sixty-three-year-old man, whereas Stanley looked like a sixty-three-year-old man who was desperately trying to look forty.

Bob Steinkellner knew in a glance that he had the wrong Trask.

He cursed under his breath, and then he tried to put a good face on it.

"All right," he said, using his best stage projection to

make sure he was heard. "It doesn't matter. I have your brother. Do you want to see him die?"

Stanley didn't answer the question. Instead, he asked one of his own: "What do you want, asshole?"

"I want a television crew. I want to tell them what you did to me."

Walter was whimpering now. He'd been left out of the conversation, as he had been left out of so many others, and he was making himself heard. "Do it, Stanley. Give him what he wants," he blurted out.

"You stay out of this," Stanley said. "This is between me and the fag."

"My name is Bob Steinkellner! Do you remember that name?"

Rush watched the exchange between the two men with cool interest. It was clear who was getting the better of it. He also watched Stegner as he took cover behind a pylon next to Rush, with his Steyr Scout sniper rifle at the ready, watching for a clean shot through the sight. Stegner had waited years to play Navy Seal sniper with that thing. Now it looked like he was going to have his chance.

"No," Stanley Trask said. "Why would I remember that name?"

"You called me," Steinkellner said, sounding like a jilted lover. "You made me buy more phones. You channel stuffed me!"

Stanley Trask laughed. "Is this to do with Feniro? That fiasco?"

A bee was buzzing around Steinkellner and Walter now, and that only added to Steinkellner's fury. "Yes, that fiasco! That fiasco ruined my life."

"Well, you got the right Trask for that. That was all Walter's idea. Tell him, Walt."

Walter's eyes bulged with fear. "Stan!" he cried.

"Go ahead, Walt. Punch him in the gut and walk off the boat. He hasn't got the guts use that knife."

Steinkellner stiffened his hold of Walter. "Try me," he said.

Then Walter went for it. He tried to break free from Steinkellner's grip and, in doing so, brought his throat, hard, against the knife. A bright rush of red blood flowed suddenly from his throat. He looked down in shock and horror as it spread south over his aloha shirt. Steinkellner drew the knife the rest of the way across Walter's throat, then looked up at them with an expression that could only be called embarrassed. The wandering bee landed on the blood as if it was honey and began to drink.

Stegner, stretched out on the deck, drew a bead with his sniper rifle. Rush kicked it aside just as he fired—the shot missed wildly. Stegner turned furiously on Rush. "What the hell are you doing?"

Rush didn't answer. He was too busy running onto the yacht.

When he got there, he found Walter Trask wiping the blood away from his throat, feeling for the mortal wound. There wasn't even a scratch.

They rushed onto the boat behind him, Donleavy, Guzman, and Stegner. Donleavy and Guzman grabbed Steinkellner, who didn't resist. He knew he was beaten.

Rush took the knife from Steinkellner's limp hand. "It's a trick knife," Rush said. "They use them in movies and in magic acts. The blood is in the blade." He pressed the blade and the center of it retracted, squirting fresh blood onto his finger. "The blood's made with Karo syrup and food coloring." He put a finger to his mouth and sucked. "Sweet. Bees don't drink blood."

Walter Trask sat on the deck, stunned. He looked up at his brother as he came on board. "How did you know—?" Walter asked his brother. "How did you know that the knife wasn't real?"

Stanley Trask gave his brother a long look. It was clear to Rush that he hadn't known any such thing.

"I took a calculated risk," he said calmly.

SIX

The Lamborghini came at them on the right, nearly sideswiping them. Amelia flew around in the back seat, trying to keep her balance, loving the thrill of the chase.

"Who are these guys?" Rush asked.

"Them."

"Yeah, but who are they?"

"I never saw them before in my life."

"They're Russian Mafiya," Rush said, keeping his eye on the road.

"What? Come on."

"Those tats. They're Russian prison tattoos."

"Why do you know that?"

Rush changed lanes abruptly. "Why are they following you?" he asked.

"They're following *you*," Amelia replied.

What could he say to that? He piloted the GTO across to the exit ramp, careening to avoid a late-model VW. Powering down the ramp, he cursed. The

Lamborghini was roaring after him. Side by side, both cars flew through a red light and down Temple Street.

The GTO peeled off to the left. The Lamborghini skidded as it tried to keep up. Rush tore through a back alley and under the overpass. The Lamborghini righted itself and was speeding to catch up. Rush took a sharp turn into oncoming traffic. Tires squealed and horns blew as cars scattered to get out of the way.

Amelia took a small object from her back pocket. A computer flash drive. She slipped it into the crease between the back of the seat and the bench for safe-keeping. She'd retrieve it later. Amelia was big believer in doing things later.

The GTO burned up the ramp onto the 110. The Lamborghini tried to follow but misjudged the turn and plowed into the yellow barrels on the median strip in an explosion of plastic splinters and water.

"Whoa!" Amelia exclaimed. "Morphin' time! Go Pink Ranger!"

Rush shook his head. "What's wrong with you?"

"I don't pay you to ask questions."

"You don't pay me at all. Now, where do you live?"

Amelia shook her head. "Uh-uh. You're not taking me home."

"Fine. I'll drop you off here."

"No. You're too noble to drop a half-naked girl off on the freeway."

"You're not half-naked."

She pulled her top off and threw it out the window

of the car. Check and mate.

◎

The GTO pulled into a garage full of rebuilt, half-built, mint-condition muscle cars from the glory days of the performance era. Firebird. Le Mans. Catalina 2 + 2 convertible. Grand Prix. These cars were Rush's passion. He labored over them for years, getting them to top condition, better than the day they rolled off the assembly line. Then he drove them for a few months. Then he sold them. The journey was the reward, as Gail said.

Amelia got out and looked around. "What is this place?"

"I live here." He tossed over an oily towel for Amelia to cover her tits. He wasn't going to let her distract him that way. "Come on."

She tied the towel around herself and followed him to the freight elevator. He slid the door open and waited for her to follow him.

She paused. He reached into his pocket, pulled out her gun, and offered it to her, butt end first.

"Make you feel better?" he asked.

She took it, but slipped it into the back of her pants. "A little."

She got in the elevator, and he slid the door down and pressed twelve.

◎

At thirty-five Zerbe still had a full head of hair. That was really all he had going for him, so he kept it long and styled like a Shakespearean actor's. He wore thick glasses and was fighting a paunch, no matter how many sit-ups he did—which wasn't many and wasn't often. Zerbe had a lot of time on his hands and spent it mostly in regret.

He was sitting in front of his computer, watching faces fly by as the LAPD face-recognition program tried to find a match for the blonde from the Nocturne, and eating a blue cheese and salami sandwich and drinking a diet root beer, when Rush walked in, followed by the pretty blonde herself. Here she was, in the flesh, with only an oily towel covering her upper half. She was even fresher and more beautiful in real life than she was in a Verizon Wireless photograph.

"Brother!" Zerbe said. "You finally brought me something home from work!"

Rush walked into his bedroom without pausing. "Don't talk to her. I'm getting her a shirt and then I'm throwing her out."

Zerbe looked at Amelia. "Well, *I* like you." He shouted to Rush. "*I* like her."

Rush moved from his bedroom to Zerbe's. "Fine, then, I'll give her one of *your* shirts."

Amelia was taking in the place. The loft's décor was Spartan. Not Spartan like *300* Spartan, with Gerard

Butler wearing a leather diaper and screaming at the top his lungs to a bunch of CGI Persians. Spartan like simple, clean, masculine. Burnished metal sliding panels divided a long, cavernous room into various spaces: bedrooms, kitchenette, living room. A large pool table doubled as dining room table on those rare occasions when Rush or Zerbe entertained. Hoods and side panels from Mustangs, Camaros, and Thunderbirds lined the walls. Martial-arts weapons—nunchakus, *tonfas,* sectional staffs, a bo, a samurai sword—served as the artwork, as did posters of Toshiro Mifune, Sonny Chiba, and Jet Li.

Amelia walked over to the floor-to-ceiling windows that lined the east wall. The non-brothers lived on the twelfth floor of the American Cement Building, a midcentury warehouse only recently converted to loft apartments. The vast windows of the building were crisscrossed with giant Xs on the outside, making it feel, Zerbe often thought, like they were on the inside of a winning tic-tac-toe game, looking out.

Amelia craned over the top V of one the Xs to see the view of MacArthur Park, a little square of black surrounded by the hideous sprawl of the not-yet-revitalized L.A. area called Westlake. It was a very convenient location. If you wanted to score crack, pick up a hooker, or buy a fake ID, all you had to do was walk out the door. Which was the one thing Zerbe couldn't do.

"Someone left the cake out in the rain," Zerbe said.

It was his standard joke.

"What?" Amelia asked, with the puzzled look that was the standard greeting to that "MacArthur Park" line. When would Zerbe learn? The ranks of Richard Harris–Jimmy Webb fans were growing thinner with each passing day.

Zerbe's command post was a bank of computers, all set into the wall for easy concealment. His usual position was right there in front of them. Despite his pasty complexion and doughy body, Zerbe cut a rather charming figure, he thought, with Stan Laurel hair and a rakish glint in his eye. He boasted five thousand friends on Facebook alone.

"What's that?" She was looking at a glass panel that was hanging from the ceiling. Projected on it was a live satellite image of Earth.

"It's off a NASA website," Zerbe explained. "The earth in real time. I call it my 'you are here' sign."

She laughed at that. It was a younger laugh than he had expected. Rush came out of Zerbe's bedroom and tossed her a T-shirt. She eyed the design skeptically. "Green Lantern?"

"'No evil shall escape my sight,'" Zerbe said, pleased that she recognized the design. "We could watch TV," he said, switching on the flat screen. An old rerun of *Wagon Train* appeared on the screen.

"We're stealing the feed from our next-door neighbor, so we have to watch whatever he watches," he explained. "He's an old guy, so he mostly watches old

Westerns and infomercials. It makes for interesting viewing."

Rush didn't want them to start bantering. He turned off the set. "Now, call yourself an Uber."

"Don't you even want to know why I hired you?"

"She hired you?" Zerbe asked.

"She didn't hire me," Rush growled. "I only work for people I like."

"That's not true," Zerbe said. "You worked for Rob Schneider. You hate Rob Schneider."

"Doesn't everyone?" he asked.

Amelia didn't like being left out of the conversation. "So you aren't even curious why someone was trying to abduct an eighteen-year-old girl?"

She was eighteen? Rush and Zerbe were silent for a moment. Then Rush told her to get the shirt on immediately.

The computer beeped, letting them know there was a match from the face-recognition program. Amelia turned to it and looked—on one half of the screen was the photo she'd taken of herself at the Nocturne that evening. On the other half was clearly a mug shot taken about six months before. She was smiling in both of them.

"What is that?"

Zerbe explained that it was LAPD's face-recognition program.

"Are you supposed to have access to that?" she asked.

"No."

"Cool."

Zerbe read the information provided. Amelia Lynn Trask. Juvie record for shoplifting, driving under the influence without a license, possession of narcotics. All-around naughty girl. Surely there was something Zerbe could repeat in mixed company. Ah, here it was....

"Stanley Trask's daughter. Isn't he in jail yet?"

"He was never charged!" she said.

Obviously he'd struck a nerve. He was about to follow up when the door to the apartment crashed in and five men in tactical assault gear burst in.

"Hand over the girl," the leader of the SWAT team said, though it took Zerbe a second to decipher it, given that the guy's voice was muffled by his helmet.

Rush didn't hesitate. He grabbed his *bo* staff and started swinging. By then Zerbe was up to speed and dashing to protect Amelia. He hadn't gone two steps when the taser hit him, exactly where you don't want a taser to hit you. It didn't knock him unconscious, but it made him wish it had.

The man who fired the taser was the first one Rush took out. Rush swung the *bo* staff and struck him just below the helmet, cracking his neck. Pivoting, he threw the whole of his weight against the staff, driving it into the Kevlar vest of another assault team member, pinning him against the wall.

"What the hell are you doing?" barked the leader,

more shocked than angry.

"I'm her bodyguard!" Rush yelled.

"What are you talking about?" The assault team leader took off her helmet. "I'm her goddamned body-guard!" Victoria Donleavy said.

SEVEN

The assault team spent a lot of time tending to Stegner, the one who'd gotten the *bo* staff in the neck. A severe case of whiplash was the diagnosis. "Wah-wah," said Zerbe. "I got a taser in the nuts and I get bupkis."

"These boys of yours need some training, Donleavy," Rush said, leaning on the *bo* staff for emphasis.

"They're fired," Donleavy growled. "Hear that? You're all fired!"

The assault team kept quiet. They were used to Donleavy's rages and knew all would be forgotten in the morning.

Zerbe kept his head between his knees and prayed for time to pass. He had a headache and a stomachache and a ballsache. He felt someone rubbing his back and thanked God for the kind touch. Turning, he saw that it was Amelia. That was even better. Now he had a headache, a stomachache, a ballsache, and an erection.

Donleavy made a call on her cell phone and reported

that Miss Trask had been located, safe and sound. She passed the phone to Amelia. "Your father wants to talk to you."

Amelia rolled her eyes, took the phone, and said "Hi, Dad," every inch the petulant teenager. "Yeah, everything's fine."

Rush shook his head at Donleavy. "I can't believe you're still tea-bagging Stanley Trask."

"It's called business," Donleavy said. "You should try it sometime."

"I'm eighteen!" Amelia cried into the phone. "What if I don't *want* to live under your roof?"

"What's her story?" Rush asked Donleavy.

"She ran off tonight. We used the LoJack in her Porsche to trace her to that nightclub where you work. We found it abandoned."

"So you thought I snatched her?"

"Let's just say it was an unlikely coincidence. We heard you'd been involved in an altercation there tonight. We posted Stegner outside your place here, just to be sure. He saw you pull in with the girl in the back seat. Naked."

"Half-naked. You got that, Stegner?"

Stegner rubbed his neck and glared at Rush.

Donleavy took the time to notice Zerbe, bent over, still clutching his chest and feeling bereft now that Amelia had stopped the back rub. "Hey, Zerbe. Do you miss prison?"

He looked up. "I miss the regular routine, but the

sodomy-free showers make up for it."

Rush moved in front of Donleavy, challenging her. "Tell me to my face you thought I abducted her."

"You're unstable," Donleavy snapped back. "You're violent! You have a grudge against the father! You fit the profile!"

"According to the threat assessment team?"

"Yes, according to the threat assessment team. And according to me!"

"She's got a gun in her pants, did you notice that?"

"I suppose you're going to tell me she abducted you?"

Amelia screamed into the phone, "I'm not coming home!" She threw the phone across the room, smashing it against the burnished steel wall. It fell in pieces on the concrete floor.

"That's my phone!" Donleavy cried.

"She has trouble with the concept of other people's stuff," Rush said.

Donleavy grabbed her by the arm. "Come on, Miss."

She pulled her arm away. "No!"

Rush stepped between Donleavy and Amelia. "I'm taking her home." Amelia looked at him in surprise. "She hired me," Rush said.

Zerbe shook his head. This was how his non-brother always got into trouble. The combination of a soft heart and a stubborn head would be his undoing one day.

⊚

Stegner and a few members of the assault team stayed behind to fix the door. They never apologized to Zerbe for the taser to his privates.

Rush and Amelia drove to the Trask house in Bel Air, flanked by two black Bonnevilles, courtesy of Tigon Security. Donleavy wasn't taking any chances that Rush might try to make a slip.

"Why aren't we in that other car?" Amelia asked, sulking. "This one's ass."

Rush had taken a 1969 red ragtop Firebird. He didn't like to take the same car out twice in row. It smacked of routine. "This baby has 440 cubic inches with Quadrajet injection. Don't you know power when you see it?"

"I know ass when I see it."

"Why did the Russian Mafiya try to snatch you?"

"They liked my butt?"

Rush shot her annoyed look. "Why are they after you?"

"I don't know."

"You want me to protect you, I gotta know who from."

Amelia was getting annoyed. "I don't *know*. All this crazy shit is going on. Ever since my uncle died."

"Your uncle died. Walter Trask?"

"Yeah, don't you read the paper?"

"Nobody reads the paper."

"He drowned himself in our swimming pool. So they say. I found him—the body, I mean. The police interviewed me and everything."

"Why'd he do it?"

"Don't you even go online?"

"Nope."

"How do you find out what's going on the world?"

"I don't."

She sighed. "All right. Our company went bust. Their company. My father and my uncle's. Biggest bankruptcy in U.S. history."

"I heard about it."

"I thought so. We're still rich and everything, but all the stockholders lost their life savings. Uncle Walter blamed himself. Got all, 'what have we done?' Then—splash."

"That's tough," Rush said. "But why would that put someone after you?"

"Oh, nobody thinks he really did it himself. Dad won't say it but—somebody whacked him."

"Whacked?"

"Killed. What do you call it when somebody kills somebody?"

"Murder."

She dismissed this with a roll of her eyes. "Anyway, that's why all the security. We used to just have one nice bodyguard at home, but he blamed himself for the Uncle Walter thing and he quit. Why do people blame themselves for stuff? I don't get it." She sighed. "Poor Tony."

"Tony?"

"Our bodyguard. Tony Guzman. It's really too bad."

Rush didn't give any visible reaction to this mention of his old friend. He just turned right into Bel Air and asked, "Why is that?"

"Tony was hot," Amelia said.

◎

Entering the Trask compound was like entering a military camp. Highly visible guards with highly visible firearms. Video cameras. Check your ID at the gate. You got your money's worth from Tigon Security.

Rush's ID didn't clear, but he had Amelia. She got him right past the guards at the front gate. The house looked like Tara from *Gone with the Wind* but bigger and more impressive. And probably with more slaves, Rush thought.

They made their way through the faux-antebellum-manor front hall and into the stage-set library, full of stage-set books, where Stanley Trask was waiting for them, in elegant silk pajamas. He hadn't changed a bit. Rush chalked that up to more plastic surgery. Surgery or no, with his thick lips, pale complexion, and snub nose, he still reminded Rush of the Creature from the Black Lagoon.

"Where the hell did you go?" Trask didn't bother with preliminaries.

Amelia answered him like any petulant teen. "Out."

Trask had to look away and swallow his anger, and

since there was nothing else to look at, he looked at Rush. "Who's this?"

"My new bodyguard," she said, defiantly.

Trask kept looking at Rush, as if there was something familiar that he couldn't quite place. Finally, to break the silence, Rush had to say something. "Caleb Rush. You remember."

A smile flickered across Trask's face. It wasn't a nice smile. "Didn't I have you blackballed?" After the incident with the hundred-dollar bills, Rush was persona non grata at every security company on the west coast.

"Yeah. Thank you for that."

That was enough attention to spend on Rush. "I'm afraid we won't be needing Mr. Rush's services, Kitten," he said to Amelia.

"Yes, we will." She was putting her foot down. "I've got Mom's trust fund. I can hire whoever I want. You should have seen him, he took out Trask's whole team like they were nothing."

"Kitten—"

"I'll sneak out of the house again! I'll go to Mom's house. *My* house," she corrected herself. "Do you want me to go alone?!"

Trask sighed. He walked out the ornate French doors onto the patio, gesturing for Rush to follow. Rush walked through darkness until he found Trask standing near the pool, his face lit by ripples of light coming from the water. He waited for Rush to him join before he began.

"I heard her screaming that night," Trask said. "I was in the pool house and I ran out and found her."

Rush could see it all. Amelia screaming. The body floating in the water. It was a lot for an eighteen-year-old to handle, even one as experienced as Amelia Trask. "Must have been tough on her."

"I wish I knew," Trask said, reflectively. Then he shook it off. "If you have a fight with me, Rush, don't come after my daughter."

"She came to me."

"Why would she do that?"

"Guzman."

The mention of the name seemed to diffuse some of Trask's anger. "Tony. When he was in his cups, which was quite often, he used to tell tales about the glory days. They often featured you. You can be quite charming in the third person."

Rush was surprised. "He drank?"

"Expertly. I demand that from my employees."

Rush was quiet for a moment, staring at the dark blue bowl of the pool. "How long did he work for you?" he asked.

"Three years. He was almost a member of the family." Trask tried to disguise it, but there was no masking the vulnerability in his voice when he asked, "Do you have any idea where he's gone?"

Rush shook his head. "But suppose Amelia thought I did. Could she have come to me to find him?"

"It's possible. She had some sort of schoolgirl crush

on him."

"Hard to think of your daughter as a schoolgirl."

Trask drew himself up. "But she is. She may act like an adult, but I assure you, actually she's a good deal younger than her years. She lost her mother a few years ago. She acts out to compensate."

Rush nodded. The man knew his daughter. It was the first thing Rush had ever found to like about him.

"Amelia's the only thing I care about," Trask said. "I intend to protect her."

"She already hired me to do that."

He looked at Rush, as though trying to figure him out. "Truthfully, did someone try to hurt her tonight?"

"The Russian mob."

"Please Mr. Rush, at least make your lies plausible. The Feds may be after me. And the IRS. But the Russian Mafiya are not among my enemies."

"Like you said, she acts like an adult. Maybe she's got a few enemies of her own."

"All right," Trask said. "If someone's going to protect my daughter, it might as well be someone vicious."

That was all the time Trask had allotted for this minor matter. He walked back to the house and through the French doors, where Donleavy was waiting. "Ah, Ms. Donleavy, would you show Mr. Rush to his station?"

Donleavy looked at Trask in surprise.

"He disabled your team, Donleavy," Trask said. "I'd rather have him on my side than on the outside. Besides, once Kitten has her heart set on something...."

When she heard that her daddy was letting her keep this stray, Amelia's squeals of joy convinced Rush that she was, indeed, eighteen.

"How's Tony?" Rush asked as Donleavy led him on a tour of premises.

"He's taking some time off. The Walter Trask thing, it hit him pretty hard."

"Maybe I should give him a call?"

"Maybe you should."

"Got his number?"

"His cell phone is disconnected. I thought maybe you'd have another way to get in touch with him."

"LinkedIn?"

Donleavy frowned. "If you do get in touch with him, tell him hello for me. Tell him...tell him I don't blame him."

"You don't blame him for Walter Trask killing himself?"

"Yeah."

"I'll tell him."

"And Crush—" Donleavy paused, awkwardly. "About this whole thing. This is a team effort. I think we both agree, you work best solo. You'll toe the line, right?"

"He never said I worked for you, Donleavy," Rush said. "You handle Trask, I'll handle Amelia."

"I'll show you to your post," she said. "If that's all right with you, that is."

Rush indicated that it was all right with him.

◎

The Donleavy team was off at eight o'clock the next morning, most of them, traipsing around after Stanley Trask as he did whatever bankrupt-and-under-investigation business tycoons do to keep busy during the day. Rush stayed in the house with the residential team. This included Stegner, who was still nursing his neck injury, and Kagan, a new recruit to the Tigon team. Kagan was a young, bullnecked ex-Marine, and Rush took a liking to him almost at once. All he had to hear was Kagan's sarcastic response to Stegner's order that he patrol the perimeter for the second time that morning.

"That's high-speed, Lieutenant," Kagan said, with admiration in his voice.

Stegner preened. He'd never served in the military, but he loved the trappings. He didn't know that "high-speed" was in fact a put-down, as was "Lieutenant." The term "high-speed" meant something that looked good but was, in reality, bullshit. And Lieutenant meant, well, Lieutenant.

"Turn to," Stegner said, using his best army lingo.

It was a little after eleven and Amelia was still sleeping the sleep of the teenage wastrel, so Rush offered to accompany Kagan on his rounds.

"You a gyrene?" Kagan asked Rush as they policed the vines around the back wall of the estate, finding a rat but no assassins.

"What gave me away?"

Kagan shrugged. "Once a Marine, always a Marine."

"And the tat?" Rush asked. "Fi" was peeking out

from under the sleeve of Kagan's shirt. The missing "Semper" was assumed.

"That cinched it."

"You should be a detective."

They were examining an abandoned aviary, which had a lot of places for ninjas to hide, but no ninjas.

"You see any action?" Kagan asked.

"Abu Hishma."

"Sweet party. I was in Baghdad for four years."

"Ah, the Green Zone. Pretty cushy assignment."

"Oh, yeah. It was just like the beach. Only without the ocean." Each knew what the other had been through. They didn't have to talk about it.

◎

Around one-twenty, Amelia came down to the kitchen and fixed herself a bowl of Frosted Flakes and a beer. "The breakfast of champions," she said, with a challenging look at Rush. He didn't rise to the bait.

"Got any Raisin Bran?" he asked.

"Didn't you already have breakfast?"

"I graze," he replied.

Stanley Trask walked in, followed by Donleavy and a phalanx of Tigon close-quarter security.

"You're up before two," Trask said to Amelia, with weary sarcasm. "I don't believe it."

"I have a big day planned," she said, tipping the bowl up to her mouth and drinking the sugar-fortified milk.

"I hope you can do all your errands online or on the phone," Trask said. "You're grounded, young lady."

She looked at him as if she'd never heard the word. "Grounded? What do you mean?"

"Tied to the ground. You may not leave the premises. You may not have any of your friends over. You are grounded."

"But I want to talk to Franklin."

The playfulness evaporated from Trask's tone. "Do you know where he is?"

"No, but his friends—"

"I don't want you to have any contact with *them*, for God's sake."

"What am I supposed to do all day?"

"Your homework?"

"It's summer, Dad."

"Do the homework you didn't do last year."

"I suppose you expect me to run off to my room and slam the door."

"I don't care what you do, just so you do it at home. You were told by Ms. Donleavy that it was not safe to go out alone. You went out. You have to learn that there are consequences to your actions."

"Isn't that what the Feds are trying to teach you?"

She scored a good point there, Rush thought, but she then spoiled it by running up to her room and, yes, slamming the door.

Amelia spent the rest of the day playing Call of Duty with some friends on the Xbox. She seemed to take great pleasure in mowing down every bald, middle-aged bystander that crossed her path.

"Who's Franklin?" Rush asked Kagan during a coffee break.

"Her big brother. He's gone AWOL."

"Anybody worried about that?"

"Trask doesn't seem to be. Franklin is kind of a black sheep."

"In this family? He must be a serial killer."

"Or a priest."

Amelia seemed to turn over a new leaf as the evening wore on. She had dinner with her father, watched season two of *Orange Is the New Black* on the big flatscreen in the living room, and said she was going to sleep at ten. She even air-kissed her dad good night.

Rush knew she was up to something. He passed Donleavy and Stegner on his way out the front door.

"Where are you going?" Donleavy asked.

"My place. I want to pick up a change of clothes and a travel bag. I don't know how long this gig will last."

Stegner smirked. "Not very long. The Trask girl gets tired of her new toys fairly quickly."

"Keep an eye on her for me while I'm gone, will you Stegner?"

Stegner looked confused. "Why me?"

"I trust you to do a thorough job."

Stegner was a bit taken aback. "Thanks, Crush."

"I'm counting on you."

With that, Rush was out the door and into his car.

He drove three times around the block before he spotted it: a Vespa hidden in the bushes at the back of the estate. He waited around the corner until half past midnight. He was beginning to think that she'd really gone to sleep when he saw the bushes move and the Vespa pull out. He waited for a respectful distance, then put the car in gear and followed her.

After all, it was what she was paying him for, wasn't it?

EIGHT

At that time of night, it only took her about a half an hour to get from Bel Air to the Venice canals. Not the Italian ones, the California ones. Dug in 1904 by a tobacco millionaire with delusions of grandeur, they originally stretched through sixteen miles of charming cottages and waterways, spanned with arching bridges. Images of graceful boating from house to house fell prey to the practicality of the automobile, and most of the canals were filled in and converted to roads in the thirties. Six blocks were spared this improvement, more from neglect than a spirit of preservation. These six blocks of algae-covered, slug-infested waterways lay hidden and forgotten by all but the beatniks and the bohemians and the hippies until the housing boom of the nineties. Then they were spruced up, scrubbed off, and dredged—and, lo and behold, one of the most exclusive neighborhoods in the greater Los Angeles area was born.

Amelia piloted her Vespa along one of these canals,

between a now-sparkling waterway on one side and fairytale cottages on the other. The houses had been built originally to identical specifications, quaint little summer cottages with porches and broad windows facing the canals, but the influx of money had recently caused them to grow as large as their footprints would allow. Only a few of the original cottages remained, dwarfed on either side by gargantuan neighbors, and it was to one of these that Amelia pulled up, doffing her helmet. The windows were blacked out from inside, but this didn't seem to bother her as she dashed up the steps, slipped a house key into the lock, and opened the door.

A blinding light from within greeted her. Rush stepped up from behind her, grabbing her arm. She looked at him with mild surprise. "Where did you come from?"

Before he could answer, an annoyed voice came from inside the house. "Sis, you ruined the take!"

It took Rush a second to adjust his eyes to the brightness that issued from the front door. Inside, the house was filled with all manner of lighting equipment, all pointing toward a poorly dressed set that Rush guessed was supposed to represent an office, judging from the desk, phone, and filing drawers. Two women in tight-fitting business suits looked toward the door in mild annoyance, which was nothing compared to the look of downright pissed-off-ness on the face of the man between them. Who was naked. And sporting an enormous erection.

Rush spun Amelia around and covered her eyes.

Amelia brushed his arm away. "Jesus, you act like I've never seen a wang before."

Rush was about to say that he didn't care what she had seen before but there would be no wangs on his watch, when the naked man started yelling at another man who was holding a high-end video camera. "Damn it, Franklin," the man yelled, his penis bobbing in time, "I thought you said this would be a professional shoot!"

The cameraman was a kid, barely older than Amelia, with red hair and freckles. He looked like Opie in a perverted version of Mayberry. From his name Rush knew that he was Amelia's brother. He defended himself vociferously. "It is! That's the Money," he said, pointing at Amelia. "Now come on, let's do this!"

The penis was drooping by now. "Aw, man, I lost my edge," the naked man said, near tears. "I'm not a machine." He turned to one of the lanky, dark-haired women next to him. "You want to help me out here?"

The tall woman rolled her eyes, grabbed her bag, and strutted toward the door. She tossed her head back to taunt, "*Raz'yoba.*"

Rush addressed her in Russian, "*Kak dela*?"

She spit at him on her way out, "*Yeb vas!*"

Amelia flipped her the finger, then turned to her brother. "What are you doing here? This is my house, remember?! Mom left it to me."

"I thought you said she was the Money, Franklin," the naked man said. Rush was starting to feel sorry for the guy, everybody ganging up on him.

"I'm family!" Franklin insisted to Amelia. "Doesn't that mean anything to you?"

"Look, are we gonna do this thing or not?" asked the naked man. Rush had had about enough. He seized the guy by the scruff of the neck and propelled him out the door and into the cold water of the canal. Then he turned to the remaining model.

"Out," he said.

The tall woman shrugged and headed out the door, pausing to say to Franklin in heavily accented English, "You owe me money."

"That much English you know!" Franklin said. The door slammed shut on her, and Franklin turned to confront Rush. "What the fuck do think you're doing?"

Rush was a big man, and when he looked at you in a certain way, he got even bigger. He looked at Franklin that way.

"Just asking," Franklin said, backing down. "Not disrespecting, just asking."

Amelia did the introductions. "This is my bodyguard. They call him Crush. This is my brother, Franklin. He makes porn. In our mother's house."

"Hey, Mom had faith in me!" he said, going around the room, switching off the lights. "Now what am I going to do? I got no content for the website. My subscribers are gonna be pissed. I got responsibilities!"

The conscientious pornographer. Rush looked at the website logo on the call sheet.

"C.F.N.M?"

"Clothed Female, Naked Male. It's the new kink. You gotta keep up with the new kink."

Amelia was shoving furniture back in place. "You messed up my stuff. Get out of my house."

Rush was tired of the playacting. "Knock it off and go ahead and talk to him, Amelia. That's why you came here, right? Sneaking out in the middle of the night. Kind of dangerous, don't you think?"

"I figured you'd follow me. That's what I'm paying you for, isn't it?" Rush's sentiments exactly. Smart girl, he thought.

"What would she want to talk to me about?" Franklin protested.

"The Russians," Rush said.

"I don't know any Russians."

"Those girls weren't talking Chinese." Rush was getting angry.

Franklin seemed to understand that it wasn't a good idea to get Rush angry, and he conceded the point. "Okay. All the best performers come from Eastern Europe these days."

"Uh-huh," Rush said. "And Tarzan Ivankov runs the Russian whores in L.A."

"They're not whores, they're actresses!" Franklin whined. "I'm a filmmaker. I'm learning my craft."

Rush picked a bullwhip up from the floor. "This is

your craft?"

"Fuck you, that's for atmosphere."

Amelia was in his face. "And whaddya mean, calling me the Money?"

"You bought the camera."

"That was for when you were going to film school. Remember that?"

Franklin made a face. "Those hacks."

"Some Russians jumped me tonight," Amelia told him. "In the parking lot of the Nocturne. Know anything about that?"

"Now I'm supposed to know about everything every Russian does in L.A." He started gathering up his things. "Maybe they just wanted some pussy, did you ever think of that?"

"I did. And fuck you."

"Fuck you too," and he was gone, out the front door.

"Nice family you got," Rush said.

"Franklin's all right," she said. "We stick together. I'd do anything for him, except he's throwing his life away."

"And you're not?"

She shrugged. "I'm just a kid."

"So this house is yours?"

"Yeah. Mom used to party with her boyfriends here. When she killed herself, she left it to me."

"Sweet story."

"Yeah. She overdosed on something. Maybe it was an accident. I like to think it was. Anyway, I spent all my time in this house before the Uncle Walter thing. Now everybody says it's 'not secure.' "

Rush moved from room to room. There were only three: living room, bedroom, and kitchen. All empty.

"So is it?" Amelia asked.

"What?"

"Secure."

"Well, as a rule a secure house is located a maximum distance from other structures, with a natural barrier of walls or trees, covered parking for vehicles, easily controlled access points...."

"So, no?"

"So, no."

She pulled a teak box from a shelf and opened it, offering the contents to Rush.

"Want some?"

"Never while I'm working."

She shrugged and rolled herself a joint. "I'm sleepy."

He stretched out on the sofa. "Get some sleep then. I'm not stopping you."

"What are you doing?"

"Protecting you. Get some sleep."

She looked at him, as if a thought just struck her. "Wanna blowjob or something?"

"Never while I'm working."

She shrugged and headed off to the bedroom.

A couple of hours later she was back. Rush was sitting on the sofa, eyes wide open, just as she'd left him.

"Don't you ever sleep?"

"Never while I'm working."

"Is that your mantra?"

"It is while I'm working."

She sat down opposite him. She'd changed into a basketball jersey and shorts.

"The Clippers?" he asked.

"Dad's a Lakers fan," she said, as if that explained it all. "So how come you can afford all those cars and that garage and everything?"

"Same as you, Mom's trust fund."

"That guy in the loft, he doesn't look like your brother."

"He's not."

"Then why...."

"You don't pay me to answer questions."

Miffed, she got up and crossed the room. "Tony said you were moody."

"I can't think of him as 'Tony.' He was always 'Guzman' on the job."

She pulled a CD off the shelf and made a face. "'Guzman' is too clumsy a name for a pretty guy like him."

Rush chuckled. "I'd love to have seen his face when you called him 'pretty.'"

She turned to him, suddenly serious. "He liked it."

Rush took that in. Guzman and Amelia Trask. Something about it didn't ring true.

She was at the CD player now, fiddling with the dials. "Hey, somebody screwed up all my settings." The CD drawer slid open.

Rush just had time to grab her and throw her across the room when the stereo exploded.

They beat the second blast, diving through the windows in a shower of shattering glass and into the water of the canal, before it tore the door off its hinges and the house went up in flames.

NINE

The house was a smoldering wreck. Cops and firefighters milled about—the cops waiting for the smoldering to stop so they could go in and do their work, the firefighters waiting for the smoldering to stop so they could go home.

Rush and Amelia sat on the ground. The houses on either side were perfectly intact, but Amelia's mother's house was just gone, like a missing tooth in a hillbilly's smile. From somewhere in the wreckage, a phone was ringing.

"It was all I had left from my mom," she said, quietly.

"I'm sorry," was all he could think to say.

"Is your mom still alive?" she asked.

Rush shook his head. "Somebody killed her."

"Who?"

"Don't know."

"I bet you'd kill him if you found out."

"Yep."

A fat guy in a suit peeled off from the group around the house and approached them. He had a nice face.

"Hey, this is your house, I understand?" he asked Amelia, like he was embarrassed by the whole thing.

"It was," she said.

"Well, yeah. I'm Detective Lambert." The phone kept ringing from inside the rubble, and Lambert turned his head barked back to the group, "Somebody find that damn phone!" Then he was back to Amelia, all concern. "Do you have any idea who that is?"

"It's probably a dissatisfied customer. My brother's website is down."

"What—?" Lambert was confused. "No, no, not the phone. The bomb. Do you have any idea who would...."

"Detective Lambert?" Lambert looked up to see two guys in much more expensive suits than his, standing there with arms folded.

"Do I know you?"

They flashed their badges. Feds.

"Agent Hendricks," said one.

"Agent Ross," said the other.

"We're taking over this crime scene," said Agent Hendricks. Or maybe it was Ross.

"The hell you are!" barked Lambert.

"This relates to an ongoing federal investigation," said Agent Ross. Or maybe it was Hendricks. "The Trask case."

Lambert swore under his breath. "Do I at least get a kiss before you screw me?"

"Assholes," said Amelia, who was apparently familiar with Messrs. Hendricks and Ross.

"Miss Trask," said one, "is this where your father kept the files?"

"Is that why you blew up the place?" asked the other one.

"What files?" asked Amelia, not entirely convincingly. "You're stupid."

"The real GlobalInterLink books," said the other one.

"The ones that'll put your father away," said the first one. "Could be on a computer or a flash drive. Could be on an MP3 player. Could be anywhere."

Rush spoke up. "I don't think this has anything to do with GlobalInterLink."

The two of them looked at him, only now acknowledging his presence. "And who are you?" asked Hendricks or Ross.

"My security man," Amelia said, proudly.

The agents looked at the exploded house, then back at Rush. "Doing a good job so far," one of them said.

Rush ignored the dig. "You ever heard of Tarzan Ivankov?"

"Tarzan?"

"Yeah, everybody asks that," Rush said. "Except your brother," he said to Amelia. "He already knew the name."

Amelia shrugged. Hendricks/Ross said, "So?"

"Ivankov runs prostitution for the Russian mob in

L.A.," Rush explained.

Hendricks/Ross quickly lost interest.

"We don't do organized crime," said one.

"Not our wheelhouse," said the other.

"Franklin Trask makes porn," Rush went on, trying to engage them. "I think Tarzan was providing the talent pool."

"Yeah, her brother's a sleaze. So what?"

"A dumb kid richer than God and the Russian Mafiya," Rush said. "Doesn't that combination strike you as a little...explosive?"

They looked over at the burned-out house. Wiseass.

"All we want is Trask," said Hendricks.

"He's a different kind of criminal altogether," said the other one.

Rush shook his head. "Thieves are all alike under the skin. Haven't you learned that yet?"

⊚

Zerbe got up early. He shaved. He showered. He even ironed his shirt. He had a very special guest coming. Raul Malo blasted from his iPod speakers.

"Walking down the boulevard, I don't need no lucky charms today!"

The doorbell rang and a vision of loveliness in beige gabardine hove into view. Frida Morales. Zerbe's parole officer.

He offered her a can of soda with, he hoped, all the

cool demeanor of a Matt Helm or a Derek Flint.

"Mountain Dew?" he asked.

"Damn it, Zerbe, I'm not your date."

"Aren't you? It's funny how fate arranges things," he said, suavely holding up a container of his urine. "My sample?"

When people asked Zerbe why he got sent to prison, he was usually too embarrassed to say corporate malfeasance. He liked to tell them he was the guy Leonardo DiCaprio played in *Catch Me If You Can*. It just sounded better.

One of the conditions of his parole was that he was allowed no access to computers or the internet. Zerbe believed that rules were meant to be, if not broken, at least strongly negotiated with. So while Frida examined the electronic tether attached to his ankle, all of his computers were safely stowed behind sliding steel walls. A place for everything and everything in its place.

"A little higher," he said, as Frida explored the burn marks on the device that would keep him tied to these four walls for three more years.

"I'm going to have to send a tech to look at this thing. Was there some sort of power surge?"

"I got hit by a taser."

She looked at him with raised eyebrows.

"Things happened," he said.

"You haven't been tampering with this, have you? This is a state-of-the-art GPS. It'll tell me the second you leave this place."

"It sees me when I'm sleeping. It knows when I'm awake."

"Don't complain. There's a new model that'll tell me whether you've been drinking. It samples the skin pores on your ankle for traces of alcohol."

"Thanks. I'll keep the tequila away from my ankle, then."

"Zerbe, you've been clean for six months," she said, patiently. "No violations, no drugs, no alcohol. Don't blow it now."

"That's right, I've been a good boy. Can't you tell them to take this thing off of me? Let me leave here?"

"You're forgetting about the six months before that."

"So I had a few slips. You could put in a good word for me. They'll listen to you. In return, I'll be happy to satisfy you like no man ever has."

Frida ignored the last part of his request, but Zerbe liked to think that she filed it away for future reference. "It would be easier if you changed the location of your custody. If you were staying with your family."

"I don't want to stay with my family. The court approved Caleb Rush as my legal whatsit."

"I think the court made a mistake."

"Hold me."

Zerbe wondered if that might have come off as needy.

When Frida left, he broke out the computers again. It was time for his online AA meeting. In Zerbe's opinion, online AA meetings were much better than real-life

AA meetings, because you could half-pay attention while playing World of Warcraft on another monitor. The only downside was, when he was asked to identify himself in the AA meeting, he had to be careful not to type "I'm Prince Darkside, and I'm an alcoholic."

He was reading Alcoholic Alan's endless dissertation on whether he missed beer more than wine, while keeping an eye out for the Corrupted Blood Plague, when Rush came in with Amelia, both of them soaking wet. Rush asked for another phone, since his was waterlogged. Zerbe grabbed one off the rack (they kept a lot of spares) and tossed it to him. He started punching in a number while Zerbe asked what happened.

"My house blew up," Amelia said, like she was reporting a bad case of termites.

"Donleavy," Rush said into the phone, "we have to talk."

◎

"So you can never leave here?" Amelia asked Zerbe, wide eyed.

Zerbe sunk the eight ball into the corner pocket, which he didn't think you were supposed to do, and said, "I'm like John Travolta in that plastic bubble."

"What's that?"

He sighed. It was just like MacArthur Park all over again. "It's a TV movie he made. Back when he was Vinnie Barbarino."

"Who?"

Kids today, he thought. They had no respect for the crap their elders used to watch.

Rush was across the room, engrossed in conversation with Donleavy, who'd rushed over to assess any damage to Amelia.

"I'm thinking you should keep her away from the Trask house," Donleavy said. "Whoever it is, he knows her routine too well."

"You think it's Guzman, don't you?" Rush asked.

Donleavy rubbed a hand over her face. She looked tired. "He knows the layout. His relationship with the family was...complex. And he's disappeared."

"Since when exactly?"

"Walter Trask killed himself two weeks ago. Guzman stuck around long enough to talk to police. Then he vanished. Even his wife doesn't know where he is."

"Or she isn't telling."

"Or she isn't telling."

Rush took a long look at the city through the window. Light was just starting to break. It looked like it was going to be a shitty day.

"What does the threat assessment team say?" he asked.

"He doesn't fit the profile."

"Chalk one up for the threat assessment team." Rush turned his back to the window. "Guzman was there on the night?"

"Yeah. When the girl spotted the body she started

screaming. Guzman ran out from the house and found her."

"Guzman did? Stanley Trask said he himself was the first one on the scene."

"Did he?" Donleavy asked.

"He implied it."

"A man like Trask is used to putting himself at the center of the story."

"And they were the only ones there?" Rush asked. "Guzman, Amelia, and Trask?"

"If you don't count Walter Trask."

"Something tells me he was used to getting left out."

Donleavy cocked an eye at Rush. "Crush, do you know why I fired you?"

"I don't play well with others? Miss Holiday said the same thing in my fifth-grade evaluation."

"Miss Holiday knew her shit. I mean, you've done all right on your own. I've kept track; I know. The way you handled the Gillespie stalker? Brilliant. I'd recommend you to anybody who was looking for one man. But you're part of a team now, whether you like it or not. So I have to ask—do you know where Guzman is?"

Rush shook his head. "No. But I gotta say, if I knew, I wouldn't tell you."

Donleavy heaved a sigh. She glanced back at Amelia. "Just find a safe house for her."

Amelia didn't notice. She was bending over the table to make a bank shot. It was truly glorious, Rush thought. The shot wasn't bad either.

"Where'd you learn to play pool like that?" Zerbe asked.

She prowled around the table and took another shot. "My dad has a table in the game room. Tony Guzman and I used to play."

Zerbe let that one go by.

"You live here, right?" she asked.

"Yep."

"And Crush...is he your brother or isn't he?" she asked as she moved to take another shot.

Zerbe glanced over to Rush and decided he was too far away to hear them. "Well, his mom was married to my dad for a while."

She nodded, understanding. "My mom and dad married a lot of people too."

"My brothers hated her," said Zerbe. "His mom. Thought she married Dad for his money. Called her terrible names. The Trophy Wife. Stripperella. The Whore."

"How come?"

"Cause she was a trophy wife and a stripper. The whore part? I don't think so. I liked her. And I like Caleb."

She looked questioningly at Zerbe.

"That's his name. Caleb Rush. He looked out for me. I was kind of a geek in high school. And this was before geeks were cool. I used to get beat up a lot. Something about me seemed to attract bullies. But once Caleb was there...well, like I said, he looked out for me."

"So now you look out for him?"

Zerbe was surprised. Few people saw that. "You noticed."

"When you love somebody, you look out for them. That's the only law that counts."

She was all right, Zerbe thought. Bending over the pool table or not.

TEN

Catherine Gail's dojo was not much to look at, a downtown storefront with a few mats and a punching bag. Just a place to keep kids off the streets and teach them about respect and tradition. If nine out of ten kids ended up falling in love with her, that wasn't her fault. She just shrugged and taught them to redirect their energy.

She was working a class full of green belts through the *katas*—Rush always thought of it as that routine the Japanese Secret Service did in *You Only Live Twice* when they were showing off to James Bond—when Rush came in, a reluctant Amelia in tow. Gail bowed to her students and dismissed them. Then she headed over to Rush. The sweat on her face only made her look more bright and glowing.

"Is this the girl?" she asked.

Amelia crinkled her nose. "It smells all locker-roomy in here."

"You get used to it," Gail said with a smile.

Amelia eyed her with distrust. "This is your teacher, huh," she said to Rush. "What does she teach you?"

"Martial arts," Rush said. "Taekwondo. Kung fu. Kallaripayattu. Savate. Judo. Muay Thai. Karate."

"So she can whip your ass."

"It's not really about—"

"Yeah, I can whip his ass," Gail said.

Rush challenged her to a sparring match. Amelia watched, bored, as Gail pulled the scarf off her head and Rush changed into some white pajamas and they went at it. Trading blows, jabbing, punching, and kicking, bouncing around on the balls of their feet, having a total blast as they sent sweeping kicks at each other's heads, spinning, twirling, blocking each other's moves with grace and style.

"You could learn this, Amelia," Gail said, panting but not winded. "There's nothing more empowering to a woman than knowing she can do this." She gave a roundhouse kick to Rush's head, just to fake him out, then spun around and let loose with a flying drop kick that would have nailed him if he hadn't moved his head just in time. As it was, the heel of her foot struck his shoulder with a blow that made him lose his footing for an instant.

"I saw that coming," Rush said with a smile.

"Just setting you up for next time," she said, grinning from ear to ear.

Amelia couldn't take it any longer. "Oh, why don't you two just get a room?!" she said, jumping to her feet and running out the door. She tried to slam it, but it was too heavy.

Stomping down the street, she didn't turn when Rush and Gail caught up with her.

"What the hell are you doing?" he demanded.

"This is stupid," Amelia said. "I don't want to be here!" Then, all at once, she was crying like a little girl. "I want to be with Tony!"

She wrapped her arms around Rush and sobbed. He looked helplessly at Gail, who pried the weeping girl off of him and led her back to the dojo.

Gail's apartment was upstairs—just a bedroom, living room, and kitchen. Nothing big, but what can you expect on a bartender/taekwondo instructor's income? Gail took Amelia up to her bedroom and let her lie down and cry it out.

Rush was pacing the kitchen when Gail came out and said she was asleep.

"You don't think Guzman would have..." Rush asked, awkwardly. "I mean, she's only a kid."

"Pretty big kid," Gail said.

He turned to look out the window. All he saw was another window across the way, with the blinds drawn. Some people were less open than others.

"I was thinking about my mother this morning," Rush said. "She did a lot of bad things."

"She did them to take care of you."

"And herself."

Gail smiled. "That girl in there, she kind of reminds

me of you. Right around the cold, black heart."

Rush chuckled. That was the reaction she'd been trying for. "Wanna fight? Best of five?" Gail asked.

Rush shook his head. "There are a couple of things I have to do first."

⊚

Stegner was standing post outside Trask's front door. It was a shit detail, and Stegner was well aware of that. There was very little likelihood, after all, that Trask's assassin would come to the front door, knock, and ask to be let in. Stegner knew Donleavy was punishing him for letting Amelia Trask slip out the night before.

That was all right, he told himself. Being given this, the most boring of assignments, was actually a blessing in disguise. It gave him time to think without the distraction of having to do anything. Stegner knew himself well enough to know he was not good at multitasking.

So he shifted his weight from one foot to the other and reasoned his way through the case before him. What puzzled him wasn't who had drowned Walter Trask and attempted to blow up Amelia Trask. Who'd done that seemed painfully obvious to Stegner. No, what puzzled him was this—why didn't anyone else see it?

Years of being with Donleavy had taught Stegner one thing—that he, Stegner, was not, in Donleavy's own words, "the sharpest tool in the shed." So why was he the only one who could see who was trying to kill Stanley Trask and his family? Could it be that Stegner was having a "hunch"? A flash of real insight? Or could it be that he was totally, completely, embarrassingly, wrong?

"Stegner?"

He was whipped from his reverie by the sight of Rush standing in front of him.

"If I was a ninja, you'd be dead by now," Rush said, smiling. Stegner really hated Rush's smile.

"Where did you come from?"

"The driveway," Rush replied.

Rush's big GTO was parked in front of the house. Stegner sighed—he must have been thinking pretty hard.

"I need to see Stanley Trask," Rush said.

"We'll see about that," Stegner said, calling in on his radio. He listened to the reply and sighed again.

"Go on. He's out back," he said as he let Rush pass. He watched Rush's big shoulders barely clear the doorway and reflected on the injustice of the world. No matter how many times Rush was slapped down, he always seemed to come back, bigger than ever. Meanwhile, Stegner always seemed to be relegated to the role of Donleavy's pet stooge.

It was time to do something about that, Stegner reflected. It was time to prove that he was a sharp tool.

◎

Stanley Trask stood on the bottom of his pool, crouched over as if scanning the cement for lost change. Somehow, pools always looked bigger when they'd been emptied of water, and to Rush, standing by the diving board, Stanley Trask seemed smaller and older as he wandered about the deep end, looking for God knows what. He reminded Rush of the Gill-Man in *The Creature Walks among Us,* separated from the water, out of his element.

"Did you lose something?" Rush asked.

Trask looked up in mild surprise. "I'm going to have it filled in. Too many memories."

Wearily, Trask walked up to the shallow end and climbed the ladder. Rush offered him a hand but Trask brushed it aside. "Where's my daughter?"

"Safe."

"No more explosions, I trust."

"Not around her."

"Then to what do I owe the pleasure?"

"I had a couple of questions I wanted answered."

Trask sat in wooden deck chair and waited. "All right."

"When Amelia found your brother, after she screamed, who came out first?"

"Tony Guzman. He jumped in and tried to save him. Too late."

"One more thing," Rush said. "Guzman. What did he drink?"

"Tequila. Patron. Want some?"

"No, thanks."

Rush looked down at the empty pool. He could see it. Guzman diving into the dark water, swimming toward Walter Trask's lifeless body. A dramatic moment.

Except Rush knew full well that Tony Guzman couldn't swim.

ELEVEN

The years had been kind to Tianna, and she didn't look any older than she had that day on the yacht a few years back, when Stanley Trask had slapped her around. In fact, she looked younger. She looked like all those years of abuse and sex for hire had never happened. As if she'd come over from the Ukraine on a work visa and actually found work as a model instead of being sidetracked into prostitution. Not that she'd had any illusions about what Tarzan had in store for her once she got to the States. She knew just what she was getting into and considered it a fair trade to reach the land of opportunity. What she hadn't counted on was it lasting more than a few years. Five max. Then she'd be on her feet and married to a rich man, supplementing her income by being a supermodel. Why not? In America, anything was possible.

Anything, unfortunately, included Tarzan Ivankov refusing to let her keep any of the money she earned until she paid back her travel expenses and visa costs.

She wasn't sure what the total amount came to, and Tarzan wouldn't tell her, but he made it clear that she'd be working for him for a long time before she made good. In the meantime, he'd be happy to loan her some money, at his rate of interest, of course. And if she wanted some drugs to ease the monotony, he could arrange that, too. For a nominal fee. The end result of this was that she was in the employ of Tarzan Ivankov and anyone he loaned her to until approximately 2035.

That was until she met Tony Guzman. Tony had been given the job of getting her weeping body home after the incident on Trask's yacht. She had shown her gratitude the only way she knew how. But unlike all the others, Guzman hadn't scrubbed himself off, thanked her very much, and left. He had stayed to talk—about where she was from and where she was going. About her dreams and aspirations. He told her about himself, too. About how his parents had made the hazardous journey from the Dominican Republic to Puerto Rico in a tiny *yola* and spent years paying the "trip planner" back for the privilege of working non-union construction jobs and changing the diapers of the offspring of the well-to-do. He'd joked about it, but she could tell it still left a bitter taste in his mouth.

And when he came back the next night, and the night after that, she didn't even think to charge him. He was a friend, and what else did she have to give? All in all, it was a nice time. When she was with other men, she just closed her eyes and imagined she was with Guzman, and the time passed much more pleasantly. But when he asked her to marry him, she had to take stock of her situation. And her situation was this: She couldn't marry anybody, because she belonged, lock, stock, and pussy, to Tarzan Ivankov.

She explained this to Guzman, teary eyed, one night and he didn't react at all like she'd expected. He knew what she did for a living. He knew what kind of pressures she was under. He also knew that Ivankov didn't want trouble. And Guzman was the kind of man who could give him plenty of trouble. So he went to Ivankov with a proposition: If he'd tell them the total amount Tianna owed him and allow them a year to pay it back, Guzman wouldn't start killing off his men. Ivankov took this with good humor, like it was a joke, and agreed. Tianna was old merchandise by now anyway. One whore wasn't worth the loss of however many men Guzman could kill.

So Guzman worked double shifts for a year, and Tianna did a few movies, and, somehow (Rush didn't quite know how) they paid off the debt. Then they got married, Tianna retired, and they lived happily ever after. Until Walter Trask went and drowned himself.

"Where's Guzman?" Rush asked Tianna when she opened her front door.

They must have been doing well the past few years, Rush thought. This little bungalow in Manhattan Beach was close enough to the water to cost a million and change. She let him in, and they sat in the dining room, with its white table and picture-perfect view of the ocean across two blocks of rooftops.

They could have done a lot of catching up. Rush had always liked Tianna, and Tianna had always liked Rush, only partly because he was one of the few men she knew who didn't put the moves on her when Guzman's back was turned. But now wasn't the time for a reunion.

"I don't know where he is, Crush," she said, and he knew she was lying. She'd never been good at faking it. That was why she hadn't made it in the movies.

"Tell him I need to talk to him," he said and left.

TWELVE

Rush sat behind the wheel in front of a rundown church on Fairfax Avenue and watched a group of middle-aged men walk out of the rectory door, chatting. One of them, with a mop of white hair above an incongruously youthful face, spotted Rush and moved to him. He moved rapidly, too, with a little skip in his step. Everything about Bill Ingol was youthful except for his age. He rapped on the window of the GTO and waited with a wry smile for Rush to roll it down.

"Caleb," he said. "Missed you at the meeting. Haven't seen you at one in a while." It was actually a long while, but he didn't have to say it.

"Been busy."

"Did you get yourself a new sponsor?"

"I'm kinda working the program on my own these days."

"Yeah. You know what they call people who work the program on their own, don't you?"

"I know. Drunks."

"As long as you know." Bill was a retired screenwriter. Retired not by choice, but by the unwritten law that if you were old enough to remember seeing the original *Star Trek* in its first showing, you were too old to write the remake.

"I'm all right. Listen—do you still sponsor Tony Guzman?"

Bill nodded.

"How's he doing?" Rush asked.

"Good. His eighth sober birthday's next month. Wanna come help blow out the candles?"

"So he's not drinking again?"

"No. Somebody say he was?"

"Tell him I need to see him. You know, if you happen to speak to him."

Bill nodded. "I'll see what I can do."

◎

Camphor-tree branches reached toward each other across the street, and the leaves met overhead, making the road into a beautiful green tunnel, but Stegner didn't notice that. The street in South Pasadena was so picturesque that twice a month it was invaded by film crews in search of the perfect suburban neighborhood. Stegner didn't appreciate that either. He was too busy casing the house across the street.

A huge Craftsman bungalow—all heavy wood beams and dark green shingles—was the address the agency had given him. Someone had spent a lot of money in the past few years restoring that big old house and, right now, a horde of eight-year-olds was doing its best to destroy it. Balloons festooned the trees, streamers entwined the porch, and a banner ran across the front of the house: HAPPY 8TH BIRTHDAY, EVAN!!!

Stegner felt a little pang as he watched the bounce house rock back and forth in the side yard. He hadn't seen his own son for, what was it, three months now? Why didn't he miss him? Was it his fault that Lydia was a total bitch, taking Richie to Connecticut without so much as a by-your-leave? What was he supposed to do? Move to Bridgeport and start over from scratch? Just so he could be close to that conniving cunt and her whining brat?

Appalled at his inner monologue, Stegner checked himself in the rear-view mirror to see if he'd grown horns and a pointed goatee. Okay, that was an evil thought. But when it came down to it, did he really feel anything but relief that Richie was out of his life? He knew that men were supposed to love their sons no matter what, but he also knew that his own father had barely tolerated him. Why should he be any different?

As he climbed out of the car, mostly to leave these taboo thoughts behind, and walked up to the house, a trio of screaming kids covered in some sugary substance nearly collided with him. A harried mother ran after them, apologizing, "Sorry! We shouldn't have done this in the front yard, but the construction...."

She didn't have to say anymore. There was always construction going on in these big homes. They reminded Stegner of the Winchester Mystery House—that place up north that had belonged to the widow of the inventor of the Winchester rifle who believed that, if she stopped building her house, the ghosts of those killed by her husband's life-work would come get her. Stegner wasn't sure what ghostly curse compelled people in the L.A. area to keep adding on to their houses, but the effect was the same.

"No problem," he said, smiling affably. "I'm looking for Justin. Do know where he is?" Stegner didn't know any child named Justin, but he felt it was a fair bet that there were as least two at this party.

The mother looked around the chaos. "Um, you might try inside. With the magician."

Bingo.

◎

Bob Steinkellner was dying. He was dying in the show business sense, since his balloon tricks had already cleared half the kids from the room. And he was dying in the spiritual sense, since he was performing magic at children's parties and living in a studio apartment off Yucca that his parole officer called "the worst piece of shit place" he'd ever set foot in. (And presumably a parole officer's feet knew shit when they stepped in it.) And, finally, he was dying in the literal sense, since he'd been diagnosed with a particularly virulent strain of follicular lymphoma, which, his doctor assured him, could be treated by chemotherapy—chemotherapy that Steinkellner couldn't afford and that he didn't really want. Right now, his full head of hair was the only blessing he had.

He finished two tricks early. The kids, looking slack-jawed and bored since they couldn't control him with a remote, ran off to beat a SpongeBob piñata to death, and Steinkellner packed his scarves and cards and Dove Pans and Chinese Wands and Rubber Ropes and Professor's Nightmare and Milk Pitcher and Needle Thru Balloon Trick and Hippy Hop Rabbits and Torn and Restored Newspaper and Mouth Coil and Egg Bag and Breakaway Wand and Magic Coloring Book neatly in his black carrying cases. He had another party to perform at in an hour. In Alhambra. Death couldn't come soon enough, he thought.

And he was only partly joking.

"Mr. Steinkellner?" The man who addressed him was a very unpleasant-looking fellow indeed. Dressed in a dark blue windbreaker, black slacks, and white shirt, he looked like a rent-a-cop who'd just taken off his tie to try to blend in with the crowd.

"Don't you mean Steiny the Magnificent?" Steinkellner replied wearily.

"We need to go somewhere and talk, Mr. Steinkellner."

"I don't think we do. At least I don't."

"How long have you been out of prison, Mr. Steinkellner?"

Steiny the Magnificent looked around—it didn't do well to let people know that their children's party entertainment was a convicted felon. No one had heard. No one was sticking around to ask for his autograph.

"You want to keep it down?" Steinkellner asked the man.

"I will. If you'll answer a few questions."

"Are you a cop? You have to tell me if you are."

"It's about Walter Trask."

"So you're not a cop. And I don't have to talk to you."

"You do if you want to avoid a scene."

Steinkellner sighed. Yeah, he wanted to avoid a scene. "Okay. I read about Walter Trask. I thought it was too bad."

"What was too bad, Mr. Steinkellner?"

"Too bad the wrong brother killed himself."

"Did he?"

Steinkellner hefted his heavy carrying cases and headed for the back door. "Look, I gotta be at the Chungs' house for little Brandon's fifth birthday in a half hour. You want to tag along, that's fine with me. Misery loves company."

"Mr. Steinkellner," the man was doing a fine impression of Jack Webb, "did you murder Walter Trask? And did you attempt to murder Amelia Trask by blowing up her house?"

Steinkellner sighed and thought about the trip to

Alhambra. Garfield Avenue would be all blocked up this time of day.

"Sure," he said. "I did it. And I was saving Stanley Trask for last. The Big Finish. Abracadabra."

◎

Rush took the coffee cup from Gail without a glance, lost in thought.

"Why would Trask lie about a thing like that?" she asked him when he told her about Guzman and water.

"Trask would lie just to keep in practice," Rush said.

Amelia walked in from the bedroom, and Rush and Gail fell silent.

"Ooh, they go all quiet when she walks into the room," Amelia said, as she poured herself a cup of coffee. "Are Mommy and Daddy fighting again?"

Gail took the plunge. "Amelia, did you and Tony Guzman have a relationship?"

"Are you my new best friend?" Amelia turned to Rush. "She's my new best friend."

"When did it start?" Rush asked.

"Three years ago. Are you doing the math? Yes, I was fifteen. Yes, he liked that. Do you think I'm getting too old for him now?" She pulled her cell phone from her pocket and checked it for messages. "He hasn't called me. What does that mean?"

"Who hasn't called you?" Gail asked.

"Tony. I did what he said. Why hasn't he called?"

"What did you do for him?" Rush asked.

"I didn't tell anybody that he killed Uncle Walter."

THIRTEEN

Rush and Gail didn't speak.

"You see, most nights I'd sneak out of my room after everybody was asleep." Amelia gave them a little smile. "You know I'm good at that."

"Good enough to fool Stegner," Rush said.

"But not good enough to fool Tony." Amelia sipped her coffee, knowing she had them on the hook, making the moment linger. "I'd go down to where Tony was on duty. At first, we'd just talk. You know, I'd go on about school and guys and my mom killing herself. Tony would talk about working and guys he'd beat up. I don't know if we knew we were flirting with each other, but we were. Every time I'd tell him about some guy I liked in school, I'd be checking him out, seeing how he reacted. And every time he told me about his wife, I could see it in his eyes that he was doing the same to me. And then he stopped talking about his wife. I knew it was only a matter of time.

"O'course there was my age to worry about, but

that was good in a way. It added to the excitement. For him anyway. Made it a real moral dilemma. Finally, he told me that I had to stop coming down. That we both knew where this was leading, and though it might not seem like a big deal to me, for him it was very big deal. I said it was a big deal for me too. Then we fucked."

She took a sip of coffee and went on.

"After that, we didn't talk so much. I'd sneak down, we'd fuck, I'd go back up. It was like we'd said everything we had to say to each other and now it was just down to doing." She smiled at the recollection and went on. "Because of that, I don't really know what was going on in his head in the days leading up to... the thing. He did seem kind of moody, now that I look back on it. When he fucked me it didn't have the same gentleness as it did at first. Not that he was violent. Just that he was throwing himself into it, as if he was trying to block something out, as if he was using sex to take his mind off something...something that was, I don't know, 'weighing on him,' I guess they'd say in books. I didn't think of that till later, of course. At the time I just thought he was getting into it. You know how guys are."

Gail nodded, because an agreement seemed to be called for.

"Anyway, this night, 'the night in question,' I snuck down like any other night. But he wasn't in the study, which was the room we usually started in. I heard splashing out in the pool and I thought, hey, he wants to do a little skinny-dipping, fine with me. I went on out. That's when I saw them in the pool. I saw Tony first, but I expected to see him. Uncle Walter I didn't expect. Not floating like that. Not all dead like that.

"Tony was struggling in water like he couldn't swim. I reached a hand out and pulled him up onto the, whaddya call it, the deck? He stood there with water streaming from his clothes and at first I thought that he'd jumped in to save Uncle Walter. Then I saw the look in his eyes."

For the first time she paused, as if at a loss for words.

"I can't tell you how I knew. I just knew. He'd killed Uncle Walter. It was right there on his face. And he knew I knew. There wasn't any point in his denying it. We just stood there, dripping water, for what seemed like ten minutes. Both of us knowing. I never felt so close to him.

"I didn't know why he'd done it and I didn't care. I told him I'd cover for him. I'd let him change, I'd let him get back to his station. Then I'd start screaming. He kissed me then. It wasn't a sexy kiss, it was a real kiss. A kiss with gratitude and love in it. A kiss that said, 'you're saving my life and I won't forget it.' He never kissed me like that before. It made doing the lying and stuff easy."

She sipped her coffee, but it had gone cold, and she made a face.

"I never got the chance to be with him after that. There were cops and shit around and everything was all messed up because, after all, Uncle Walter was dead. And then Tony disappeared. But that was okay because I know he had to, whaddya call it, 'lie low' for a while, and I respect that. But why the hell doesn't he *call*?"

◎

Usually Rush put on the gloves before he started pummeling the punching bag in Gail's dojo. Hell, usually he carefully wrapped his hands with Everlast Super Gauze, *then* put on the gloves. Better safe than sorry. But that night was different. That night he just started wailing away at it, bloody knuckles be damned.

"Somebody in there you don't like?" Gail asked after watching him deliver a jab, straight right, right uppercut, and left hook to the bag. It was a killer combination, and the bag had nothing to offer in defense.

He stopped, out of breath, sweating through his street clothes. "How old were you when you lost it, Gail?"

"You don't think I'm still a virgin, Caleb? That hurts."

"But when you were underage, did you ever have anyone hit on you? An adult, I mean."

"That's what I love about you, Crush. You're big, you're mean, and you're totally naïve."

Rush's cell phone beeped before he had the chance to respond. He went to the bench to pick it up.

"It's a text message for Amelia."

"On your phone?"

"I forwarded her calls to me."

"That's dirty."

"It's not hard if you know how to do it. I'll show you sometime."

"It's still dirty."

Rush shrugged and thumbed the phone to read the message. It was short and to the point, and it was from Tony.

I miss you

He flipped the phone shut, opened it again, and called Zerbe's number.

Zerbe was having a little time to himself with the computer and didn't relish being interrupted.

"Zerbe," Rush said, instead of hello.

"Great timing, man," Zerbe said, exasperated. "You totally cock-blocked me."

"Who's there?"

"Nobody. That's how I knew I was going to get lucky."

"Buy yourself some flowers later. I need a favor. I need you to zero in on a mobile number. Now."

"Cool." This was interesting. Zerbe wiped the lotion off his hand and got down to business.

"I'm forwarding you the number."

"Do you know his carrier?"

"No."

"More of a challenge. I'll have it for you in a sec."

He switched off his phone and turned to Gail. "I

gotta go. You'll be okay?"

"What do you mean?" she asked.

"There are people looking for her. They might be dangerous."

Gail gave him a look. "I can whip *your* ass, can't I?"

FOURTEEN

Stegner couldn't believe his luck. He'd followed up on a hunch and it had paid off. While everyone else was chasing shadows, he'd pursued a simply obvious line of inquiry to its logical conclusion—the guy who had tried to kill Trask before was trying to kill him again.

Steinkellner was dictating his confession into the voice memo gizmo on Stegner's iPhone while Stegner drove him back to Trask's mansion. He was to be presented to Donleavy with a big fucking bow around his neck. Now who was the sharpest tool in the shed, you fat bastard?

A thought struck Stegner—he really should call Donleavy and tell her where he was. The only thing was, Steinkellner was using his cell phone to tell him how he'd gotten the explosives into the house in Venice and wired them to explode on cue.

"Could I use the phone for a minute?" Stegner asked.

"I'm just getting to the good part. You want me to lose my flow?"

"I'll just be a second."

Steinkellner shrugged and handed him the phone, making sure his voice memo was saved. He was pretty much done anyway.

Stegner hit Donleavy on his speed dial.

"Where the fuck are you?" This was Donleavy's special greeting.

"You'll be happy when you see me."

"I'll be happy to fucking fire your ass. You were supposed to be watching Trask."

"No need to watch him. He's safe now."

"Yeah, he's safe. Since Kagan tracked him down."

"He left the compound?"

"You'd know that if you'd been watching him."

"Where did he go?"

"To his office. Downtown. Kagan found him shredding documents."

Stegner turned onto Beverly Glen. "It's doesn't matter."

"The fuck it doesn't matter."

"You can pack up and go home. I've—" Stegner stopped himself on the verge of saying "I've solved the case." That sounded so clichéd. But hadn't he?

"You've what? Go home, Steg. I don't want to see you again."

"You'll want to see me."

Steinkellner listened to Stegner on the phone and was reminded of the time he'd briefly gone out with a girl who was very much out of his league. He spent the whole time pleading and threatening and negotiating, but it was a lost cause. They both knew he'd never rise to her level.

Steinkellner felt sorry for Stegner but sorrier for himself. He had accomplished so little in his brief existence on this planet. But at least, he thought, he'd go out with a bang. He could see the headlines on TMZ now. "Mastermind of the Trask Family Tragedy Dies." There was only one thing left to do. Die.

Ta-da!

Stegner was done with his call, so he offered the phone back to Steinkellner, who brushed it aside. "I'm pretty much done."

"Really?"

"I need a break. You'll figure the rest out. You're a smart guy."

Stegner smiled with satisfaction. "I was smart enough to catch you."

"Indeed you were. Hey, want to see a trick?"

"What?"

"A magic trick. An old standard. Hey, watch that light." He added this last part in an offhand way, to get Stegner to look away. Steinkellner took advantage of his distracted glance at the traffic lights to slip the mouth coil between his jaws. Presto-chango. Misdirection. Steiny still had it.

While they were stopped at the red light, Steinkellner gestured and got Stegner's attention. He displayed his empty palms, and then he started pulling an endless stream of paper from his mouth, accompanied by the requisite expressions of astonishment. *How on earth is he doing that?*

Stegner laughed. "How on earth are you doing that?"

Then Steinkellner swallowed the mouth coil.

He kept pulling the long strand of paper as he began to choke and turn purple.

"Hey," Stegner asked, "is this part of the trick?"

The mouth coil was small enough to fit in Steinkellner's mouth but large enough to block his windpipe. Look, Ma, no air!

Stegner threw the handbrake on and reached over to Steinkellner to try to dislodge whatever was stuck in his throat, but all he could do was pull out more streams of paper. He tried to slug Steinkellner in the stomach, an improvised Heimlich maneuver, but all that did was make the poor guy choke more.

Then Steinkellner stopped choking altogether, his face turning a dreadful shade of blue. Stegner got out of the Lincoln, ignoring the honking of the cars backed up behind him on Beverly Glen. He rushed around to the passenger seat and flung the door open. Steinkellner flopped out like a dead fish, only his seat belt stopping him from hitting pavement.

He was dead. Just like that. Abracadabra?

Stegner cursed his fate. And then he remembered that he still had the confession on the cell phone in his hand. Thank God. He called 911, while the car horns blared and traffic backed up all the way to Ventura Boulevard.

If there was one thing Steiny the Magnificent knew how to do, it was how to make himself disappear.

FIFTEEN

Rush called Zerbe from the GTO, barking into the Bluetooth in his ear. "What have you got for me?"

"Whoa, slow down. It's not so easy to triangulate a cell phone, despite what you see on TV. You want your miracle, you'll have to wait for it."

Rush hung up. Two minutes later, he called again.

"What have you got for me?"

"I cannae change the laws of physics, Captain." Zerbe thought doing a little Scotty from *Star Trek* would relax Rush. It didn't. Rush hung up, and two minutes later he was calling again.

"What have you got for me?"

"You got that playing on a loop?"

"Come on. He's gone to ground. Help me out here."

This time Zerbe had something for him. "Got it. Downtown. Figueroa and 4th Street." In other words, the Bonaventure Hotel. That was going to ground in style.

The Bonaventure's gleaming glass towers sat in the

middle of downtown L.A. like a movie set from the seventies that escaped into real life. It was big, it was brash, and it dwarfed the buildings around it, even the ones that were taller. Rush always thought it looked like a spider, lurking among the downtown skyscrapers, looking for a meal.

Within ten minutes, he was standing in the huge atrium, looking up at the elevators as they climbed up, up out of sight. It took a big building to make Rush look small. The Bonaventure filled the bill.

He called Zerbe. Again. He was working out with his Wii Fit. He put it on pause.

"What's up now?" Zerbe asked.

"I'm gonna text Guzman a reply. I'm gonna tell him I want to see him."

"Why will he want to see you?"

"He won't. But he'll want to see Amelia."

"Okay. Not hard," Zerbe said. "You got your number blocked, right?"

"Yep." Rush thumbed the keypad on his cell phone, typing a message.

"Wait," Zerbe said. "If you want him to think it's from Amelia, don't spell out words. Use numbers, letters. 'I want 2 C U.' Like that. The number 2, the letter C. You know?"

"Why?"

"Come on, just pretend you're an eighteen-year-old girl."

"I don't have a lot of experience with that."

"That's right, you were never in prison."

Rush sent the message. Then he settled down with a coffee to wait for the reply. He had his pick of five coffeehouses in the sprawling atrium—he picked the Krispy Kreme doughnut shop. Quality first.

With a box of a dozen hot glazed in front of him, he was prepared for a long wait. Then his phone rang. It was Donleavy. He sighed and answered.

"What's up?" he said, sipping the hot coffee.

"We're out of a job."

"Pardon?"

"Trask is letting us go."

"He's developed a death wish?"

"Apparently we got the guy."

"Who?"

"Bob Steinkellner. You remember him."

"I don't believe it."

"He confessed. Then he offed himself. By choking on a magic trick."

"Says who?"

"Stegner."

"Jesus. You buy this?"

"No. The police aren't sure either. But Trask is. We're packing up and moving out."

"Okay."

"But you don't work for Trask. You work for the girl."

"That I do."

"There's something going on, and I don't like it.

Don't let that girl out of your sight."

Donleavy hung up before Rush had a chance to respond. He thought it over long and hard while he ate six doughnuts, and he hadn't made any sense of it when his phone buzzed. He flipped it open and read the message.

2 dangerous.

He called Zerbe. "He says it's too dangerous. With a '2.'"

"Say please," Zerbe said while drinking a Fanta. "With two Es and a Z. And a smiley face."

"I don't do emoticons."

"You'll do it for me."

He did it.

And the reply came in short order.

Where/when?

And Rush texted back, *Grand Central Market. Now.*

A little bit longer for this reply, but it came.

OK

The elevators of the Bonaventure Hotel were its most famous features. Running outside of the building, on parallel tracks, they provided a spectacular view of the city, as well as a spectacular view of each other. Ask any exhibitionist.

Rush checked the number display on the elevators—they were both coming down. He positioned himself between the two, ready to move to either one. The elevator to his right arrived first. The doors opened, disgorging a full load of passengers. Rush scanned the faces of the strangers as they came into view, looking for Guzman's familiar smile.

Instead he saw Franklin Trask, Amelia's pornographer brother. Franklin was the last one out of the elevator, and he looked like he hadn't slept since Rush had seen him leaving the house in Venice.

Franklin did a sort of stumbling double take when he saw Rush, as if it took a second to recognize him, and then when he did, he wasn't happy. Rush gave him a smile. "Good 2 C U," he said. It wasn't the kind of smile to set Franklin at ease.

Franklin looked as if he were about to speak, then he thought better of it and took a dive back for the elevator. Rush would have caught him, but just as he moved, a family of four passed in front of him, luggage piled high on a carrier. He darted around them and got to the elevator just as its doors closed.

He pivoted on the balls of his feet and dashed for the other elevator. It had just emptied itself of its passengers and he was able to get in, throw a single, startled businessman out, and press UP.

The sparkling nighttime skyline of the city was spread out all around him, but Rush only had eyes for that other elevator, half a floor above him. Through the glass walls, he could see its lone passenger. He pulled out his phone and made a call.

Franklin gave a little helpless shrug in his elevator and answered his phone. "Hello," he said warily.

"Hey, Franklin, what's up?"

"Damn it! Damn it, damn it, damn it!"

"How'd you get hold of Guzman's phone?"

"Damn it!"

"And using it to set up your sister? That's not nice."

"Damn it! He just wants to talk to her."

"Who?"

Franklin didn't answer—he just stomped his foot on the elevator floor like a kid having a tantrum. Which was what he was, after all.

"You know the difference between the Italian mob and the Russian mob, don't you?" Rush said into the phone. "Piss off an Italian, he'll kill you. Piss off a Russian, he'll kill you and your family."

"It's not like that," Franklin pleaded. "Ivankov just figured it would be easier to talk to her if she was away from there."

Rush felt a chill wash down his spine. Did Ivankov know where she was? "Away from where?"

"He just wants to talk to her."

"Those people don't talk. Do they know where she is?"

Franklin didn't answer.

"How do they know where she is?"

"She texted me. So I wouldn't worry about her. We're close that way."

"Did you tell Ivankov where she is?"

"I might have mentioned it."

Franklin's elevator came to stop before Rush could answer. The door slid open, and Franklin moved to the side to make way for the new passengers. Two Russians came in. Rush recognized one as the guy with tattooed rings on his fingers from the encounter outside the Nocturne. Rings grabbed Franklin and took his cell phone. The second guy held up a gun and blasted through the glass wall of the elevator. Rings shoved the startled Franklin through the shattered glass and dropped him.

Rush could just see Franklin's face as he passed him on the way down. He looked surprised. Rush supposed that would pass and there would be time for surprise to be replaced by a lot of other feelings between now and when he hit the pavement. *Can you believe that?* he seemed to be thinking. *I didn't see* that *coming.*

"Crush," a voice spoke in Rush's ear. It took Rush a second to realize that it was coming from his Bluetooth.

"Yeah," he answered.

"Good, it is you," the voice said in heavily accented English. "My friends will meet you on the next floor."

SIXTEEN

"Colonel Mustard in the Conservatory with the lead pipe."

Gail looked at Amelia, as if considering speaking, and then she showed her the card with the lead pipe on it. It was Gail's turn. She rolled. Damn. Only four. She still had to get to the hallway. She moved her red piece four spaces, and then she handed the dice to Amelia.

Amelia put them down without rolling and said, "Colonel Mustard in the Conservatory with the lead pipe."

This time Gail spoke. "You already guessed that."

"I know," Amelia said, flatly.

"You already guessed that twice."

She shrugged and said, "Colonel Mustard in the Conservatory with the lead pipe."

"Why do you keep saying that?"

" 'Cause I think Colonel Mustard did it. With the lead pipe. In the Conservatory."

"I showed you the lead pipe."

"I know."

"Before that I showed you the Conservatory."

"I know."

"Then why—"

"How do I know you're not an accomplice? How do I know you two aren't in cahoots?"

"Look, if you don't want to play...."

"I want to play. I want to solve this crime. I want to find out who killed Mr. Body. You're the one who's crapping out on this. What exactly do you have to hide?"

"Amelia...."

"Once again I ask: Colonel Mustard in the Conservatory with the—"

There was a crash from downstairs. Gail was almost relieved to hear it—it meant a distraction from dealing with this angry, young, and extremely annoying girl. She gestured for Amelia to be silent and moved to the door.

As she slipped silently down the hall, Gail reflected on the probable causes of the noise down in the dojo. It might be the neighborhood kids trying to kick in the window and rob the place, for instance. They did that a couple of times when Gail first moved in, but she'd caught them at it and given them a few lessons in street fighting. They pretty much left the dojo alone after that.

On the other hand, it might be a panicked raccoon trying to find a safe haven from the city streets. That had happened once, too, and Gail had trapped it, fed it a can of tuna, and sent it on its way. Strays had to stick together.

Or it might be a gang of Russian goons trying to take Amelia. You just never knew.

When she saw the big men rushing up the stairs toward her, Gail had her answer. She took a split second to acknowledge that before knocking the lead one out with a leaping sidekick to the head and sending him tumbling back onto the others. How many others there were, she couldn't say. She stopped counting at seven.

She thought of turning and running. She thought of yelling a warning to Amelia. She disregarded those thoughts immediately. When you're on the run you can be caught. When you cry out a warning to someone, all you do is let the hunter know they're close to their prey. No, the only thing to do when being attacked was to attack back. Harder.

She knew she could hold them off for few minutes at best, enough time for Amelia to hear them breaking up the place and slip out the back window to the street before they took Gail down. True, Gail was probably a better fighter than any of them, so if they attacked her one at a time, the way they did in the movies, she could whip them all and finish by standing victorious over their broken bodies. But as she dived into the tangled mass of Russian mobsters, she realized they probably had seen those same movies. They wouldn't make the same mistake as Bruce Lee's assailants or

Chuck Norris's assailants or Jet Li's assailants or Jason Statham's assailants. They wouldn't stand and wait their turn. They'd take her all at once.

Fucking reality.

SEVENTEEN

"My friends will meet you on the next floor." The man with the skeleton tattoo (whose name was Sergei) listened to the man with the ring tattoos (whose name was Danzig) on his Bluetooth and rolled his eyes.

That was supposed to be Sergei's cue to take action, he thought, facing the elevator doors with that hulking lunk Semyon by his side. But did Danzig have to deliver it with that Blofeldian smirk? Not for the first time, Sergei wondered what kind of *bratva* he had gotten himself into.

Sergei hadn't even wanted to be a gangster. It was just the only way he could get from Tkibuli, that west Georgian shithole he was born in, to Los Angeles, where he could realize his dream. To be Phil Spector.

Phil Spector of the Wall of Sound. Music producer extraordinaire, yes. Also the Phil Spector who could pick up a blonde at the House of Blues, take her home to his castle in Alhambra, have sex with her, blow her brains out, and get off with a mistrial. That was the high life, no question.

Sergei loved music, mixing sounds and beats together and making them collide, almost as much as he loved killing people. Maybe more. And that was saying a lot. Because killing people, watching the life go out of their faces, hearing their last breath, that really got Sergei's juices flowing. But to combine the two, music and death? That took balls of bronze.

True, Spector had been convicted on the second pass, but by then Sergei was already in L.A., indentured to Tarzan Ivankov. As a henchman. Sergei had been unfamiliar with the term till one of Tarzan's whores called him that. He'd slapped her (open handed—he wasn't *that* mad) when she used the word, because it didn't sound complimentary. He asked her what it meant, and since she was an American whore from Canada, unlike most of Tarzan's stable, she was able to explain: "It's like one of those guys in an action movie that works for bad guy and gets shot and nobody minds." So that was what a henchman was. Interesting. He hit her again, this time with his closed fist. Still, she had a point, and he felt a little bad about it afterward.

So he was a henchman, Sergei thought. Okay. For now. You had to start somewhere. He spent his spare time in clubs, listening to all the lousy bands and imagining fixing them, making them better, giving them the Wall of Sound.

"It's here," Semyon growled the obvious, as always.

The elevator doors slid open. They had to be quick about this. People were already gathering in the street around the body of that prick Danzig had dropped out of the other elevator a floor above them. Danzig, with his damn ring tattoos (a ring for every man he'd killed, as he'd explained far too often for it to be cool), had perhaps taken too literally Tarzan's order to "put him down." No matter. Danzig was running down the service stairs now, trying to get outside before the cops got here and the building was sealed. So the lowly henchman were given the next assignment: Kill this man they called Crush, the man who'd done so much damage to them in the parking lot of the Nocturne. Kill him in the elevator quickly and efficiently and get out.

But when the doors opened, the elevator was empty. Sergei stepped in, looking all around, and then turned back to look at Semyon, who looked as puzzled as Sergei was, when the elevator doors started to close. Sergei reached out to stop the doors when an angry two-hundred-twenty-pound bald man dropped down from the sky on top of him.

Crush.

As the door slid shut, Sergei noted that although he had looked all around for someone, he hadn't looked up. Rookie henchman mistake, he thought, as Crush rained his fists down on him.

◎

As Rush was beating this Russian mobster to a pulp, taking the gun from his hand and beating him some more, he noticed something. The man wasn't fighting back. Rush paused as he recognized him. Skeleton Tat. From the club.

"You all right?" he asked, in Russian.

"You win," the man answered in a thick Georgian accent. Eastern Europe Georgia, not southern U.S. Georgia. Though both had their coal mines. And from the look of this man's hands, he knew them well.

"That's it?" Rush asked.

"Yeah...don't kill me."

"You were going to kill me."

"Just doing my job."

"It's a lousy job."

"Tell me about it."

"Well, I'm not going to kill you."

"Thanks."

"You'd still kill me if you had the chance, though, right?"

"Well, orders. You know."

The elevator doors slid open. "Tenth floor. You get off here." Rush half rolled, half pushed Skeleton Tat out of the elevator. "I'll tell Tarzan you put up more of a fight."

"I don't fight when I know I'm going to lose. Waste of energy."

"Wise man," Rush said as the doors closed.

It took an eternity to get down to the garage level,

where the police were just arriving. They were just starting to shut the building down but hadn't yet gotten to the service entrance. Rush ran through it, his heart pounding in his chest. He had to contact Gail. He had to know if she was all right.

As he ran to the car on Flower Street, he dialed her number furiously on his cell phone. It rang and rang, until her voicemail answered. He called again and again. Always with the same result.

He started the car and sped down Flower, turning onto 4th as he called the police and told them there was an assault taking place at Gail's dojo. The officers would probably get there before him, so if he was wrong, if Gail and Amelia were working out and she was just letting the machine take the calls, Gail would make Rush do Palgwe forms till the sun came up. But if he was right....

It took him six and a half minutes to get there, dodging traffic, tearing through red lights. Pulling up in front of the dojo, he saw that the front window was busted in and the cops were nowhere in sight. LAPD, to serve and protect—in their own good time.

Rush ran through the broken plate-glass window, calling out, "Gail! Amelia!" No answer.

The dojo had been wrecked. Benches overturned, mirrors shattered, punching bag slashed. Rush didn't pause to assess the damage. He just ran up the stairs, flipping the light switches as he passed. They didn't come on. The bulbs had all been shattered.

The kitchen was untouched and empty. He heard faint music coming from the bedroom down the hall. Walking toward it, he checked the closet. Empty. He checked the bathroom. Empty, but the sink was filled with bloody water, and bloodstained towels were strewn around the room. Gail hadn't gone down without a fight.

The bedroom door was closed. He swung it open with a lump in his throat. The room was in shambles. The bed was turned on its side, the card table was tossed into the corner, the Clue game board and pieces scattered around it—a rope, a knife, a lead pipe, a revolver—like so much evidence in a tiny crime scene.

Gail's iPod was plugged into its speakers. Belle & Sebastian were playing. "It's been a bloody stupid day...."

There was a card on the windowsill, where he couldn't miss it. It was Miss Scarlet. Gail's favorite. Across it was scrawled a phone number.

"Don't leave the light on, baby," the iPod sang. Anger flaring in his gut, Rush snatched the iPod from its cradle and made to throw it across the room. He stopped himself just in time. For the sake of Gail's playlists.

He took a deep breath, then pulled out his cell phone and dialed the number that was written on the card. Slowly and deliberately. He didn't want to enter the wrong numbers.

The phone rang. And rang.

Then he heard it. The faint sound of a cell phone ringing somewhere nearby. In the apartment.

He followed the sound. Followed it downstairs. Followed it across the darkened dojo to the equipment closet in the corner. *Dear God,* Rush thought, *don't let this be what I think it's going to be.*

EIGHTEEN

Rush hadn't screamed since he was a child. That was during the bad times, when his mother had to turn tricks in their one-bedroom apartment off Cherokee and she'd lock him in the closet with a blanket and pillow and tell him to keep quiet till it was over. One time he'd heard her panting and struggling and gasping for breath, as if someone was strangling her and pounding the hell out of her at the same time—which, he later reflected, was basically what was going on. He knew he had to help her. So he'd screamed at the top of his lungs and pounded on the door. How his mother had whipped him for that!

Of course, it wasn't nearly the whipping she'd given her john when he suggested little Caleb join them for a three-way. A mother bear protects her cubs even if the mother bear is selling her ass on Hollywood Boulevard.

So that was the last time Rush screamed, and he didn't scream now as he looked in the closet. He just gave out a low, blood-chilling moan.

Gail was in there.

Her body was crammed into the corner of the closet. Twisted and bloody, like a piece of boxing equipment used and then tossed away. The ringing cell phone was duct-taped to her naked chest. A piece of butcher's paper was taped across her face—another phone number was scrawled on it. The paper moved, sucked in by her breath.

Ripping the paper from her face, Rush bent down to her. Her breath was shallow and fast but it was there.

"Gail," he said. "It's going to be all right."

She mumbled something. Rush couldn't quite make it out, but the sound of her voice made his heart leap.

She tried again. "There were too many of them, Crush."

"Must have been a hundred," Rush said, holding her gently.

Gail snorted a laugh. An actual laugh. "Five or six. They took her. I'm so sorry." She started to cry, and Rush held her to his chest, shaking with relief.

Sirens approached. In a minute, red flashing lights would wash through the room, and he'd be stuck there for hours, answering the same questions over and over, while *they* were out there laughing about what they'd done to Gail and what they were going to do to Amelia.

Gail looked up at him. "Go," she said. "Go get her."

⊚

Rush stood in the shadows across the street long enough to see the paramedics load Gail into an ambulance. Then he pulled the wadded-up paper from his pocket and called the number scrawled on it.

A harsh, accented voice answered. "Took you long enough."

Rush kept his voice even. "My friend needed a doctor."

"You mean she isn't dead? *Chyort*!"

"Where's Amelia?" Rush asked.

"Where's Guzman?"

"I don't know."

"I call this phone in two hours. That's ten o'clock. If Guzman doesn't answer, we kill her."

"I—"

"And don't involve anyone else."

"If you hurt her—"

"Oh, we've already been hurting her."

The line went dead. Rush ran toward the car.

◎

Philippe's was busy. The legendary sandwich shop was always busy. Had been since 1908. How many places in L.A. could say that?

Rush tromped across the sawdust-covered floor, past the long wooden tables filled with old-timers and new-timers, pushing through the line at the counter to where Bill Ingol was working, carving roast beef and pork for the multitudes. As Bill used to say at AA meetings, carving meat wasn't that different from screenwriting.

"We need to talk," Rush said.

"Take a number like everybody else," Bill replied.

Rush snatched a number from the hipster standing next him. The hipster almost objected, but one glance from the big, angry man made him retreat under his porkpie hat. Discretion, after all, was the better part of cool.

Bill took a cigarette break in the alley out back by the dumpster. Rush didn't have time for preliminaries. He told him that he needed to reach Guzman.

"I'm his sponsor, not his goddamn message service."

"This is life and death."

"What isn't?"

Rush grabbed him by the collar and shoved him against a brick wall. Bill didn't flinch. He'd dealt with worse trouble before.

Feeling guilty, Rush relaxed his grip. "I'll start going to meetings again."

Bill smiled. "Now you're talking, Caleb."

"So where is he?"

Stubbing out his cigarette, Bill said, "He's at home, genius. That's where he's been all along."

◎

Rush skidded to a double-parked stop in front of Guzman's Manhattan Beach house, ran up the steep stairs, and hammered on the door.

"Guzman!" he yelled.

He tried the door. It was unlocked. Flinging it open, he rushed inside.

"Guzman!"

He heard a sound coming from upstairs. A woman crying. Rush took the stairs three at a time and burst into the guest bedroom.

Tianna was sitting on the floor by the unmade bed, sobbing.

"Where is he?" Rush asked from the doorway.

She looked up at him, bereft. "He said he didn't love me anymore."

Rush didn't have time for this. "Where did he go?"

"I don't know," she wailed.

He went into the master bedroom. Tianna followed him in as he flung open the door of the huge walk-in closet. "What did he take with him?" Ripping through the closet, Rush searched for he didn't know what.

Tianna sniffled. "He's in some kind of trouble, Crush."

"How do you know?"

"Because he loves me. He wouldn't lie unless...."

There it was. An open lockbox on the floor of the closet, with a few loose papers inside. He picked it up.

"What was in this?" he asked Tianna.

She wiped her eyes. "Papers. Birth certificates, our

passports."

He took out the only passport from the box. "*Your* passport."

He threw the lockbox on the bed and headed out. She scuffled after him, whimpering. "Where are you going?" she moaned. "What do you know?"

Rush stopped on the landing. The view of the ocean from the picture window was stunning.

"What do *you* know?" he asked. "How the hell can you afford this place? Did you go back on the job?"

"No! I'm clean! Tony paid me off! I'm free and clear."

"How? How did he get the money?"

Tianna grew silent.

Rush pressed. "Did he do a favor for Ivankov?"

"I don't know. All know is, Ivankov said I was free."

"Do you think a man like Ivankov would ever let you be free?"

"You don't know him. He's a man of honor."

"I don't have to know him. I know his kind."

"Ivankov gave me his word. In the Thieves' World, honor is everything."

Rush turned on her, intensely. "Don't talk to me about the Thieves' World. I know it better than you. If you think you're safe, you're wrong. Run. Go someplace no one has ever heard of you. Lock your door. Never leave."

"But Tony—"

"You've lost Tony. We all have."

Tianna watched him go.

NINETEEN

Rush sped around the traffic circle to Shell Avenue. He thought he could make it to the L.A. airport in fifteen minutes. He had twenty-five left. Twenty-five minutes till the Russians called back. Twenty-five minutes till Amelia died.

As he tore onto Venice Boulevard, he reflected on the idea that the world probably wouldn't be a worse place without Amelia Trask. She was a spoiled-rotten and naturally perverse creature who would no doubt make many men very unhappy in her adult life. Still, when he thought of what the Russians had done to Gail, it made his blood boil, and he wanted to do the same to them, only worse. And if he saved Amelia, he might be able to get his hands on them.

He called Zerbe as he turned right onto Lincoln. His roommate was no help.

"You want to know what flight Guzman's on, but you don't know the airline or where he's going?" Zerbe was irritated. "What, do you think I'm one of those guys in *24* with a magic computer that can tell you *everything*? In 3-D?"

"The Dominican Republic. He's going back home."

"All right. That gives me something. I'll call you back."

He was on 96th Street before Zerbe called him back.

"You can't get there from here."

"What?" Rush was in no mood for jokes.

"You have to fly to Miami and catch a shuttle to Punta Cana or Santa Domingo."

"Fine. Who flies to Miami?"

"Delta has the only red-eye."

"When does it leave?"

"Ten thirty-five."

"Thanks." He ripped the Bluetooth out of his ear as he turned into LAX. Traffic slowed—he watched the time ticking away. Twelve minutes to ten.

He pulled up to the curb and quickly divested himself of the things airport security would frown on. A Glock pistol. Two knives. A Beretta. A pair of brass knuckles. These he deposited under the passenger seat. From a false back in the glove compartment, he withdrew an envelope he kept for emergencies. Then he jumped out and ran. Delta was in terminal three, and he was at terminal one, but he could get there faster on foot.

True, he didn't know if Guzman would be there. Maybe he was driving down to San Diego and through Mexico. Maybe he was taking a flight to somewhere else. Hell, maybe he was taking a Greyhound bus to Canada. But it was something to do while the time ticked away. Something to do while he waited for the phone in his pocket to ring.

Rushing through the sliding doors, he threaded through the crowd, looking around for the security checkpoint. Upstairs. If Guzman was here, he'd undoubtedly already passed through it, into the impregnable security of the terminal. Only one way to get inside.

Rush waited an interminable six minutes in the ticket line, then rushed to the counter when the clerk gave him a bored nod. His turn.

"One ticket to Miami."

"I'm afraid that flight is fully booked. Would you care to try standby?"

"Sure."

Rush suffered as the clerk clicked an impossible pattern of numbers on her keyboard. Then she said, "I'm afraid standby is fully booked."

"Can I have a ticket on the next flight?"

"To Miami?"

"To anywhere."

She looked at him blankly. "Pardon?"

"Yes, to Miami."

Another series of relentless clicks. "That flight doesn't leave until 11:35 a.m. tomorrow."

"That's fine. I'll curl up with a good book and wait."

He had no intention of getting on the plane. He just wanted to get through the fucking security line.

Ripping open the envelope he'd pulled from the glove compartment, he dumped out a wad of hundreds and bought the ticket.

Upstairs, the security line was mercifully short. He shifted from one foot to the other, the blood pounding in his head, as the old lady in front of him got a good feel-up from the TSA agent. Then he ripped off his shoes, dropped the cell phone in a tray, peeled off his jacket, and stepped into the X-ray booth, arms held above his head. The machine beeped.

Cursing under his breath, Rush submitted to a wanding and a pat down from an acne-scarred security guard. His wristwatch was the offending object. He stripped it off and went through the whole procedure again. This time he passed.

He snatched his possessions from the conveyor belt, stuffing the watch into his pocket, snatching up the envelope with the remaining hundreds, not caring who saw it. *Just let someone try to mug me tonight,* he thought.

Lastly, he plucked the cell phone from its little plastic tray. Just then, the phone rang. It was ten o'clock. Shit.

TWENTY

Tony Guzman waited in line to get on board Delta Flight 108 to Miami. His ticket said he was in boarding group four, which meant he'd be among the last people on board, so there'd be no room in the overhead compartments for his carry-on. He didn't care. All he was carrying on was his passport and five thousand dollars taped to his chest. "Travel light and they can't lose your luggage," Walter Trask used to joke.

Wincing at the memory, Guzman thought again about Walter Trask and his death. It was so stupid, so senseless. So messy. He closed his eyes and tried to think of happier thoughts, but none came to him. He closed his eyes tighter and tried to figure out what the hell he'd do in Punta Cana when he finally got there. Apply for a job working security in one of the resorts? That was the first place Ivankov would look for him.

When he opened his eyes again, a very big man, panting like he'd run a marathon, was holding a cell phone in front of his face.

"Talk!" the big man demanded. It was Rush. Guzman had been found.

"I got nothing to say," Guzman replied.

Rush shoved the phone closer to his mouth. "Talk!"

Realization dawned on Guzman's face as he heard the all-too-familiar voice on the other end of the line. "Are you there, Tony?" Ivankov.

Guzman grabbed the phone. "I'm here."

"Say something more—let me know it's really you."

Guzman gritted his teeth. "Sometime, when you least expect it, I'm going to stick a knife up your ass and watch you bleed out."

Ivankov laughed. "That's the Guzman I know. Is that Crush-man there?"

"Yes."

"Let me talk to him."

Guzman passed the phone back to Rush. "He wants to talk to you."

Rush seized the phone. "Ivankov?"

"Very good on the first round, Mr. Crush. Ready for level two?"

"No more games—"

"I'm texting you an address. Be there in twenty minutes, both of you, or I kill her. I'll kill her the way Guzman said he was going to kill me. Sound like fun?"

At that, the call went dead.

Rush turned to Guzman. "You have to come with me."

Guzman shook his head. "No."

"They have her."

Guzman looked stricken. "Tianna?"

"Amelia Trask."

Guzman groaned. "That girl can take care of herself."

"They're going to kill her."

"Let them. Let them kill that whole damn family. They're crazy. All of them."

The plane was boarding. Guzman moved toward the gate.

"You think Tianna is safe if you're not with her?" Rush asked. "You're wrong. Trust me—if they can't find you, they'll find her. They already got Gail."

Guzman hesitated. "Is she...?"

"She'll survive. I hope. They won't."

"What do you mean?"

"I want to take them on."

"Jesus, Crush."

"We can do it together."

Guzman gave it a long thought. "No, we can't."

Rush grabbed him with his big hand. Guzman was a big man. Rush was bigger.

"Guzman, listen to me. Whatever you did, it's over. They will track you down. They will cut off your balls and make you watch while they carve up Tianna with a chainsaw. Your only hope is to take it to them. You know that."

Guzman stood still for a moment, as if petrified by the image. Then all at once he was on the move, heading back down the terminal, fear replaced by, or at least disguised as, determination.

Rush had to run to keep up.

"What does Ivankov have against you, anyway?" he asked.

Guzman gave a mirthless laugh while he ran. "I introduced him to Stanley Trask."

TWENTY-ONE

Victoria Donleavy left Kagan in the car with Stegner and took one more walk around the house. This was partially to check to see if they'd left the Trask place spic and span, but mostly so she didn't have to listen to Stegner crow about how he'd "cracked the case."

Stegner hadn't cracked the case. The police didn't think so. The FBI didn't think so. Donleavy and Kagan didn't think so. Hell, the gardener didn't think so.

Nobody thought so.

Nobody except Stegner and Stanley Trask.

Donleavy found Trask in the gym. It looked like the sort of gym you'd find in a five-star hotel: weight equipment, an inversion table, an elliptical trainer, a number of treadmills, all lined up by a window overlooking the estate. Had the executives all worked out together here in the halcyon days of Trask's empire? If they did, Donleavy would bet they'd always kept one eye on Trask and did one less repetition than he did. The alpha dog always had to be first.

Trask was on his back, bench-pressing what looked like two hundred pounds without breaking a sweat. Donleavy knew she was supposed to be impressed, but she just couldn't muster it.

"Mr. Trask."

"Just a sec." Trask lifted the weight and set it in the uprights without asking for Donleavy to spot him. She knew she was supposed to be impressed with that, too. Maybe he wanted her to come on to him. Christ, she'd be glad to see the last of this guy.

"Yes?" Trask said, making a point of wiping himself down.

"I'll be bidding you farewell, Mr. Trask." Donleavy got formal at occasions like these.

"Oh. You did a good job. I'll be sure to recommend your firm to anyone who asks."

"Goodbye, Mr. Trask." Donleavy turned and walked toward the door. She stopped. "You know he didn't do it, right?"

"Excuse me?"

"Steinkellner."

"He confessed."

"His confession was bullshit. And you know that."

"Do I?"

"Why do you want us to leave, Mr. Trask?"

"I don't need you anymore."

"Is that because you don't need protection? Or because you don't want people around to see what you're doing?"

Trask leveled one of his deadly stares at Donleavy. She knew the stare: the one that was guaranteed to scare the shit out of his underlings, to make hard-boiled executives shiver in their Gucci loafers. Hell, it had even scared her once or twice. But not anymore. Trask wasn't her boss now. He was just a little man who probably mislabeled his weights to make himself seem stronger than he was.

"That will be all, Ms. Donleavy."

"You can throw your life away, Mr. Trask. I really don't mind. But what about your daughter? Don't you care what happens to her?"

At this, Trask finally lost it. Years of being in control had sat comfortably on him, and the loss of it wrenched him, made him shout out, made his voice break like a teenager.

"Get out!" he croaked, tears forming in his eyes.

Donleavy had to look away. Would wonders never cease? She actually felt sorry for Stanley Trask.

TWENTY-TWO

Rush was barreling down La Tijera Boulevard and trying to read the text on his iPhone, but the GTO was bumping too much. He really needed to check the suspension. Rush handed the phone to Guzman.

"Can you read that?" he asked.

"854 North Almadero Street. You know where that is?"

Rush pulled a thick book out of the car door pocket and tossed it to Guzman. "Look it up."

"You still have a Thomas Guide?" The Thomas Guide was the old map bible every driver had to have in Southern California, circa 1990. "What about GPS?"

"GPS knows where you are."

"Still staying off the grid, Crush?"

"You'll thank me later."

Guzman flipped to the index and found the page with the street on it. "It's near Olvera Street. Christ, we'll never make it."

"I know a few short cuts," Rush said, taking a right on Angeles Vista. He checked the dashboard clock. It read 10:08. They had twelve minutes.

"Stanley Trask said you were drinking again."

"Christ, all this is going on and you're going to bust me about boozing?" Guzman asked.

"Bill Ingol said you were clean."

"I lied to Bill."

"You lied to your sponsor. Why the hell would you do that? What does that get you?"

"I lied to a lot of people."

"Tianna?"

"If you can't lie to your wife, who can you lie to?" Guzman said with a mirthless laugh.

"Why lie to anybody?"

"I'm not as simple as you are, Crush. Nobody is. People lie. They lie because they want somebody to believe they're better than they really are. They lie because while they're lying, they can believe it, too."

"What started you drinking again?"

"Stanley Trask liked to drink when he talked. I liked it when he talked to me."

"What did you two talk about? You killing his brother? And banging his daughter?" Rush tore through a red light on to Martin Luther King, squealing and swerving to avoid oncoming traffic. "Were you really screwing that kid?"

Guzman shifted uncomfortably. "Haven't you ever done something you're not proud of?"

"Yeah, but I'm not proud of it."

"But I certainly didn't talk about that with Stanley

Trask."

"What did you talk about?"

"I didn't talk about anything. All I did was listen. That was all he wanted. That was all *I* wanted." Guzman sighed. "I was in the house all the time, Crush. I heard everything. Information, it was just lying around."

"Is that what this is about? Insider trading?"

"You just had to look at their faces and you knew when to buy, when to sell. It didn't seem like anything wrong."

The traffic came to a stop, and Rush slammed on the brakes, threw it in reverse, and spun the wheel, cutting down to Broadway.

Guzman didn't pay any attention. He was in confessional mode, letting it pour out of him, trying to make sense of it. "The Trasks didn't mind. They'd been bleeding the company dry for years. They didn't care if I fed a little from the trough. I think it made them feel big."

"Bigger?"

"They couldn't get big enough. At least not Stanley. But then it all started going to hell. All those people lost their life savings. And Walter, he started falling apart."

"Developing a conscience?"

Guzman shrugged. "If you want."

Rush gunned it down Washington. It was 10:18.

"He was ready to go to the SEC," Guzman continued. "Confess everything. Take the noble way out. And everybody would get sucked down with him. Including me."

Rush hit gridlock on Los Angeles Street. He swore and looked behind him. It was like a parking lot back there. He twisted the wheel and bumped up onto the sidewalk, scraping his fender on the concrete K-rail and flying over the curb onto Almadero.

"So that's why you killed him," Rush asked, "to stop him from going to the SEC?"

"I didn't kill him," Guzman said.

"Are you lying to me to make you feel better about yourself?"

Careening to a stop right in front of a dingy warehouse on Almadero Street, Rush checked the clock. 10:19. A minute to spare.

"We're here," Rush said.

"What do we do now?"

"Now we walk into a trap."

TWENTY-THREE

The dilapidated warehouse loomed above them. It was the perfect place, Rush thought, for a gang hit. He got out of the car and Guzman followed. The elephant doors in the front of the warehouse were open just a crack. The darkness and silence from within hit Guzman like a sledgehammer after being tossed around in the GTO, so he hung back.

Rush walked around to the passenger door and rooted around under the seat. He came back with a Beretta and a Glock and offered them to Guzman. Guzman took the Beretta. Given a choice, Rush knew, he'd always pick the heavier gun.

"So how does Ivankov fit in to all this?" Rush asked.

"Stanley Trask found out I knew Ivankov. He thought it would be cool to know a gangster. You know, psychopaths like to hang together."

"Do they?"

Guzman shrugged. "I don't know. Actually, they didn't like each other. I think they were too much alike.

Except that Ivankov had a little bit more sympathy for people he whacked. Mostly the two of them just sat around measuring their dicks."

"Literally?"

"One time, yeah. Stanley won. Man, was Tarzan pissed about that. In the end, though, they just talked shop."

"And?"

"That's it."

Rush was about to ask how two middle-aged men sitting around talking about work could lead to two murders, an attempted murder, a bombed house, and a kidnapping when he was interrupted by a cell phone ringing.

Instinctively, Rush and Guzman checked their phones. The ringing wasn't coming from them.

It was coming from inside the warehouse.

"Hit the lights," Rush told Guzman, tossing him the keys. Guzman got into the car and switched on the headlights. The beams hit the elephant door enough to illuminate the shadows within and make them look, if anything, more ominous.

"Wait here," Rush told Guzman as he walked toward the darkness and was engulfed by it.

Eyes adjusting to the blackness inside, Rush could make out only a few cars parked in the vast expanse of dusty emptiness. A Cadillac. A Bonneville. A couple of Volvos.

The phone kept ringing with an annoying chirpy

sound, like the factory default alert on a cheap cell phone. He couldn't find the damn phone anywhere.

"We're here!" Rush shouted, his voice echoing off the cement and bouncing back to him. "Damn it, we're here! Where are you?"

The phone kept ringing. He'd run the gauntlet from LAX to here and made it in time—but it was all for nothing because he couldn't find the goddamn phone.

Rush spun on his heels, calling out to Guzman, "Shut off the headlights."

"What?"

"Shut them off!"

Guzman complied, and the garage plunged into darkness. Rush waited a moment. The phone rang again. And with it, a faint green light pulsed from underneath the Cadillac.

Rushing across the warehouse floor, Rush dove underneath the Caddie. The cell phone was there, secured with duct tape to the undercarriage. He ripped it free and answered it just as the last ring echoed through the warehouse. Then the words appeared on the screen: ONE MISSED CALL.

They were too late.

TWENTY-FOUR

Tarzan Ivankov hit the "end" button on his iPhone the second he heard Rush pick up on the other end. At least he assumed it was Rush. It might have been Guzman. It might have been some drunken homeless person who wandered into the warehouse and saw the phone blinking. It didn't matter. He'd wait for the person to call back. Then he'd get things started.

Ivankov was a bear of a man—covered with a thick mat of hair from his toes to just below his startling blue eyes. His head was totally bald, a fact that used to irk him no end. In America, body hair was not in fashion, while head hair was considered the young man's mark of virility. He could have waxed his body thoroughly and got himself a toupee. He'd considered it. Then he figured, fuck it. *Let me be a bear,* he thought. *Let me be a gorilla. Let me be Tarzan of the Apes.*

He put the phone in his pocket and flicked on the cattle prod that he carried like a walking stick. It was one of his trademarks. Along with his bald head and hairy body. It was all part of a carefully calculated attempt to give himself an image. A legend. A mystique.

He walked across the vast expanse of the top floor of the warehouse on Almadero Street. Nothing but exposed pipes and whitewashed windows, just a few pieces of furniture: a Barcalounger and flat-screen TV attached to the wall to make it homier. It was one of Ivankov's safe houses. He had dozens of them around town, and he kept them as austere as possible, to make them more threatening to his people. No reason to make them feel comfortable anytime, anywhere.

No reason to make Trask's daughter feel comfortable either. He stopped in front of a dog crate, a wire cage that came about up to his belt buckle, so that he had to bend down to look inside. Amelia Trask was in there, curled up like one of the pit bulls he used to raise for dog fights. She raised her head and met his gaze. But she wasn't scared, not the way she should have been. She looked angry instead.

He flicked the switch on the cattle prod and stuck it between the wires of the cage, right into her flank. She let out a howling scream of pain. That was a little better. But there was still too much anger behind the pain. He'd have to break her of that.

The cell phone rang again. He yanked it from his pocket. "What do you want? I'm kind of in the middle of something."

"We're here, damn it!" The angry man on the other end of the line must be Rush.

Ivankov chuckled. "You're too late."

"You want something? We're here."

"Do you have it?"

A pause on the line, then Rush said, "Of course."

"The last man who lied to me has to have his mom wipe his ass for him."

"My mother's dead."

"My condolences. Take the freight elevator to the top floor. I'll be there."

"And Amelia Trask?"

"She'll be waiting for you." Ivankov hung up and smiled at Amelia.

"How 'bout that, *sucka*? Your boyfriend's coming to rescue you."

"Kiss my ass!" Amelia snapped.

"Show respect!" he howled back, and he stuck the cattle prod through the cage, zapping her again until she screamed. Kneeling down on the concrete floor, he peered in at her. She was afraid. That was better, he thought with a smile.

"I'm gonna wreck you," he said.

The rumbling sound of the freight elevator climbing to the top floor started to drown him out. Ivankov stood up irritated, then called out an order. "Here they come! Get ready!"

The three henchmen waited: Semyon, Sergei, and Danzig. They raised their Gewehr 36-C assault rifles and took aim at the elevator door.

The elevator rose and ground to a stop behind the

wooden slats of the sliding door.

There was a pause.

Then the doors split apart and a Pontiac GTO crashed through them and sped out into the middle of the room.

TWENTY-FIVE

Five minutes earlier:

"My mother's dead," Rush said into the phone.

"My condolences," Ivankov replied. "Take the freight elevator up to the top floor. I'll be there."

"And Amelia Trask?"

"She'll be waiting for you."

And he hung up.

Rush looked across the garage and saw a huge freight elevator waiting for him with its sliding door open like an angry mouth.

He turned and looked out at the GTO, parked on the street.

⊚

The wooden slat doors of the old freight elevator splintered from the impact as the GTO crashed through them and the car charged into the warehouse like a bull released from a pen.

Ivankov's men scrambled. Sergei dived out of the way as the car wheeled around the room. Danzig collected himself and let loose a barrage from his Gewehr that pelted the side of the Pontiac. Guzman rolled down the side window and fired his Beretta.

Semyon opened fire from the other side of the room as Danzig dove for cover. Bullets struck the outside of the car and smashed the windshield into spider webs. Rush was glad he'd installed the bulletproof glass, but those bullets really were screwing up the paint job. This car was going to be a total loss.

Guzman leaned out the window, still firing, just as Rush saw the big hairy man, who must have been Ivankov, pick up a Mossberg 590 riot shotgun. A mean piece of work, both the man and the gun. Rush threw the car in reverse and planted his foot on the accelerator, smashing into Danzig on the way, throwing him across the room.

Rush slammed on the brakes and put the car in drive, wheels skidding on the concrete floor, steering the GTO right for Ivankov.

Ivankov dived to one side and the car missed him. Scrambling to his feet, he ran toward where Amelia was still crouching in her little cage. He opened the door and dragged her out, betting that Rush wouldn't plow into them both.

Rush did a three-sixty and spun around till the car

was pointed straight at Ivankov again. He gunned the motor. He was playing chicken. But both Rush and Ivankov knew who had the upper hand.

An impact shattered the side window and Rush turned to see Semyon firing at him.

Guzman leaned out the window and took a shot at him. Semyon fired again, got lucky, and hit Guzman in the right forearm. The gun flew out of Guzman's hand and he fell back in the seat, crying out in pain.

The GTO took off, Rush at the wheel, barreling straight at Ivankov. At the last minute, Rush spun a 180 and tried to take out Semyon. Sergei was laying down steady fire with another Gewehr, and Semyon jumped into the elevator for safety.

Unfortunately, the elevator had returned to the ground floor. Semyon sounded surprised all the way down.

Rush spun the GTO around and spotted Ivankov again.

He had the shotgun pointed at Amelia's head. "Get out of the car!" he shouted.

Rush sat behind the wheel, staring at Ivankov. Ivankov stared right back at him. Neither blinked.

Rush looked over at Guzman, who was slumped in the passenger seat, clutching his bleeding arm. He sighed. They had no other options. Rush turned off the engine.

"Take the keys and drop them out the window," Ivankov said.

Rush took the keys and dropped them out the window.

"Get out!" Ivankov said.

Rush opened the car door, stepped out, and slammed it shut behind him. Guzman got out of the car, too, although in his case it was more like a fall. He kicked the door shut and slid to the concrete floor.

Ivankov smiled, victorious. He swung the shotgun around and fired at Rush.

A rubber bullet hit Rush square in the chest, and he fell back from the impact.

Ivankov smiled and turned to his surviving henchmen.

"String him up!" he said.

TWENTY-SIX

Donleavy hesitated before ringing Stanley Trask's doorbell. Their parting had been final, irrevocable, and, to be honest, rather insulting to Donleavy. She'd told herself, as she walked away, that if Trask ever called her again, she'd tell the bastard to fuck off and hang up on him.

But when she'd returned to the office and her secretary said there was a call from Stanley Trask, she took it. A girl had to make a living.

"Yes," she said, with just enough edge to her voice to let Trask know she wasn't happy.

"Victoria...."

"Yes, what is it?" Nobody called Donleavy by her first name.

"I...I may have been too hasty." Trask's voice sounded odd. Was he actually afraid?

"What's the matter?"

"Just...can you get down here? Right away?"

"Yes, of course, but—"

The call cut off. She grabbed her keys and headed back to his house. On the way, she called Trask repeatedly on his cell phone, on his house phone, on his business line. She got no answer.

Still, when she reached his door, she hesitated. *Why?* Was it that Trask had made her eat shit and now was bringing her back for more? Or was it just that she didn't want to see his ugly fish face again?

She rang the doorbell. And waited. She rang again. And waited.

Her cop instincts kicked in. She drew her Smith and Wesson from her holster and tried the door.

It was unlocked.

She threw the door open walked in, gun at the ready. No one there. She searched the house.

No one anywhere.

Until she got to the gym.

The maid was lying in a pool of blood by the elliptical machine. Her breathing was raspy, and the crack in the back of her skull was bleeding profusely.

Donleavy called 911. She lifted the maid's head and put her jacket under it. Next to the maid, a heavy kettle bell lay on its side, the bottom of it flecked with blood.

The maid's eyes drifted open.

"Do you know who did this to you?" Donleavy asked.

The maid shook her head, feebly. Even that movement was too much for her and she cried out in pain. Donleavy held her steady.

"It's all right. The ambulance is on its way."

"What about Mr. Trask? Is he all right?" she asked.

"Yeah, he's fine," Donleavy lied.

Whoever had hit her on the head must have taken him. Trask was gone.

TWENTY-SEVEN

When it came back to him, Rush's vision was foggy and blurred, like he was looking at everything through a smeared pane of glass. His breathing was hard and ragged and labored. He felt pain in every muscle.

And then there was the fact that someone was punching him repeatedly in the kidneys.

Rush tried to shake his head, hoping that might clear his vision, but his head weighed too much to shake. As he drifted further into consciousness, he became aware that his arms were chained to a rusted pipe over his head and that something was tied to his face. A pair of goggles and a respirator—the kind worn by men working in hazardous environments.

"Good, you're awake," Ivankov said.

Ivankov was standing in front of him, holding a limp sock filled with something. Rush tried to move toward him and realized that his feet were tied, too—bound tightly together with his own belt.

Rush looked around. A couple of the Russians were sitting on the floor, nursing their wounds. Amelia was crouching in a small wire crate, stuffed in there like an animal. But she still had her clothes on. Rush took that as a good sign. Guzman was chained to the same pipe as Rush, bleeding from the bullet hole in his arm and, blessedly, unconscious. And Rush? He couldn't see himself, but he guessed he didn't look much better.

He did notice that no one else was wearing a respirator, so that told him there hadn't been a gas leak. No, the respirator was on him for another reason.

Ivankov walked up to Rush and tapped on his face mask with the butt end of a lit cigarette.

"Where is it?" Ivankov asked.

Rush didn't respond.

Ivankov held up the sock, which drooped over his fist. It looked like a blackjack.

"You know what this is?" Ivankov said. "It's a sock filled with dirt. In the Russian prisons, you had to make do."

He stepped around to Rush's back, swung the sock back, and struck him hard on the kidneys. Rush groaned.

"Where's the flash drive?" Ivankov asked.

"What flash drive?" Rush said, his voice muffled by the respirator.

Ivankov struck again, harder this time. "Where is it?"

Rush twisted wildly against the bonds. "I don't know," he lied.

Ivankov hit him again. "Where is it?"

"Did you check your pockets?" Rush asked. "Lots of times, when I misplace things—"

The sock, again. Harder.

"I'm talking about the flash drive that has all of Trask's books on it," Ivankov said. "The real books. The ones that incriminate me. Tell me where it is."

Rush felt faint from pain. He nodded his head toward Guzman. "Ask him. I thought he was the one you wanted."

Guzman hung from the pipe, unconscious. Or pretending to be.

"Oh, I did want him," Ivankov said. "I'll get to him. But I don't want him to tell me anything. I just want him to feel pain. You have to tell me something. Where is it? The bitch told me she gave it to you," Ivankov said looking over to Amelia. Her eyes were wide.

"I had to give it to him!" she said. "He made me! He tortured me!"

Rush didn't blame Amelia for lying. In a few minutes, he'd be telling Ivankov anything he wanted to hear.

Ivankov laughed. "Torture. That word gets thrown around a lot these days." He reached out to the valve on Rush's respirator and turned it, cutting off his air. "Let me tell you what torture is," Ivankov whispered.

Rush started to panic as he tried to suck in oxygen and got nothing.

"It's not humiliation," Ivankov went on. "That's just embarrassment. That's fucking *life*. No, torture is pain.

Crippling, destructive pain. And along with it, the hope that somehow, some way, you just might survive. Hope is the real torture."

Rush began to struggle, to twist on his chain.

Ivankov watched with great interest while Rush's face turned red and then blue.

As Rush bucked against the restraints, tiny pinpoints of blood began to appear in the whites of his eyes. His body shuddered and he passed out.

Darkness....

The darkness was quiet and comforting and oh so still. It felt so good to rest. It would be good to rest forever....

Then it started again. The THUD, THUD, THUD—the dull pain in his kidneys. He had thought he'd left pain behind.

Rush experienced wrenching pain as the respirator was ripped from his head, and then all-encompassing agony as his lungs spasmed and filled with air. It felt like a hundred knives were being plunged into his chest from within.

Rush opened his eyes. Ivankov was standing in front of him, holding the respirator.

"It felt like dying, didn't it?" Ivankov said with a smirk.

"Made a nice change," Rush tried to mumble. He wasn't sure if the remark was audible, but it made him feel better to try to say it.

"I could do it again," Ivankov said. "Or this."

Ivankov recommenced beating Rush's kidneys.

"I can do this all night. You'll be pissing blood for a month. If you ever piss again. Dead men don't piss, eh?"

Rush gritted his teeth. He refused to cry out. Not crying out was the one way he had of maintaining control over the situation. It wasn't much, but it was something.

"You think you're strong enough to take this?" Ivankov said. "You're not."

He twisted Rush around on his chain to see Guzman hanging next to him, bloody and unconscious.

"He wasn't."

Ivankov twisted Rush back to face him. "You know why I wanted him? Because he did me a favor. Favor that bit me in the ass. Now look at him!" Ivankov's breath tasted hot and fetid in Rush's mouth.

"My grandfather used to carry an anvil around on his back in the old country. Just for fun. The Ministry of Internal Affairs took him. They broke him. They made him their bitch."

"Otvali!" Rush said and spit in Ivankov's mouth. *Otvali* meant "piss off" in Russian. Rush was getting tired of all this.

Ivankov struck him again with the blackjack.

"Where did you learn Russian?" he asked.

"Vor v zakone," Rush said. From the Thieves' World.

Ivankov's eyes widened. "What do you know about the Thieves' World?"

"More than you, *sucka*!" Rush spat. "Look at my heart."

Ivankov considered...then ripped the T-shirt off Rush's chest. His ribs had an ugly purple and yellow bruise from the impact of the rubber bullet, but that wasn't what made Ivankov take a sharp breath. It was the tattoo beneath it that shocked him. The elaborate tat covered Caleb Rush's entire chest and was executed with homemade precision in needle and ink instead of an electronic machine. It depicted a grinning skull with a knife in its jaws, tears falling from the empty eye sockets, manacles hanging from the blade. Behind it all, rising like a mushroom cloud of destruction, was the onion dome of Saint Sophia Cathedral in Kiev, cracked and bleeding like a boxer who'd taken too many blows to the head.

Ivankov didn't say a word. He pulled a Ka-Bar knife from his boot, as if to defend himself from the ghastly image.

"Who carved this on you?"

"My father," Rush said. "Blaz Kusinko."

He might as well have said his father was Jesus Christ. "I should cut this off your skin," Ivankov said.

Rush's eyes locked with his. "I'd thank you for that."

Ivankov laughed. He turned to his henchmen, who were sitting against the wall, happy to let Ivankov torture away so they could rest.

"Blaz Kusinko!" Ivankov said to them. "Sergei, Danzig, have you ever heard of him?"

They didn't know how they were supposed to react. One nodded and one shook his head. One of them had to be right.

Ivankov was disgusted. "Punks today. They have no respect for history. He was one of the founding fathers! The first boss of Brighton Beach. In the seventies. Ancient history, I suppose. Came straight from the gulag, thank you Perestroika. Those were the days. Started the Russian mob here in America. And you know how he died? Peacefully. In bed. With one of his whores." He cocked an eye toward Rush. "Was your mother one of his whores?"

Rush just stared at him.

"Look!" Ivankov laughed. "Look how proud he is! His mother must have been a good whore!"

The Russian strutted around Rush like a runway model.

"That's how I'm going to die too," Ivankov said. "Not in prison for some pissant white-collar crime! Not because I hooked up with her crazy family." Ivankov spit in Amelia's direction.

Rush started laughing. "You invested in Global-InterLink?"

That struck a nerve. Ivankov stamped his foot like an angry three-year-old. "I did not! I just wanted to put my money somewhere safe. So I could retire with dignity. And then this one...." He socked Guzman's unconscious body like a punching bag. "He introduced me to the fucking Trasks!"

"Is that the favor he did for you? Is that why you hate him?"

"Isn't that enough? Oh, the Trasks, they liked me at first. I was their pet Goodfella. I got to pimp for her brother. Tell them the stories about my wicked ways... and in return they gave me tips, they gave me info that only they knew. Places to invest." He turned to shout in Rush's face. "What's illegal about that?!"

"It's called insider trading," Rush replied, calmly. "Ask Guzman about it."

"So what? Everybody does that! I am not going to prison for that. Not after all the things I've done!" He grabbed Rush by the hair and shoved the respirator back on his head, yanking it in place. He put his fingers back on the air valve. Smiling, he turned off Rush's air.

Rush tried not to panic. "So that's why you're going to kill Guzman? And that's why you killed her uncle?"

"I didn't kill her uncle. I just killed her brother."

Amelia looked up at him, shocked.

"Now, I'm asking you one more time," Ivankov said, staring into Rush's eyes. "Where is the flash drive?"

Rush couldn't help trying to breathe. His lungs strained. The world began to blur.

Ivankov opened the valve and Rush sucked in air. Blessed air. If he lived through this, he was going to thank God every time he inhaled.

"Ne znayu," Rush said, not because he was trying to be clever, but because he was lapsing into the tongue of his childhood. *I don't know, Momma....*

Furious, Ivankov grabbed his cattle prod from the rough wooden table and zapped Amelia with it. She screamed.

Rush yanked against his restraints.

Ivankov laughed at Rush's reaction. "Ooh, you don't like that! You're not Kusinko's boy. He loved watching girls scream. You squeamish about that, Crush?" He turned to one of his henchmen and barked. "Sergei, put her on the table."

Sergei unlatched the crate, pulled Amelia out by the hair, and threw her onto the wooden table.

"I heard what old Blaz used to do with his whores when they stepped out of line. It was ugly." Ivankov laughed and turned to Rush. "But I bet your mother liked that. You know, I probably screwed your mother. I screwed a lot of Kusinko's whores. What was left of them."

"It's in the car!" Rush said. Ivankov looked at him. "The flash drive," he went on, "it's in the back seat of the GTO."

Ivankov eyed Rush, suspiciously. "Where?"

Rush jangled the chains that held his wrists. "It'll be easier if I show you."

Ivankov picked up a Glock from a pile of weapons in the corner. He leveled it at Rush. "Now why should I do that?" He gestured to Sergei. "Get it."

Sergei moved to the door of the car and reached to open it.

"I wouldn't do that," Rush said. "I got a little tired of

people breaking into my cars. I made it so that anyone but me who opens it gets a little surprise."

Sergei hesitated.

"Go on, Sergei," Ivankov barked. "He's bluffing."

Sergei reached for door. He stopped. "Why would he be bluffing?"

Ivankov let out an exasperated sigh. "Why would he tell us?"

"All right," Rush said. "But don't be mad at me when he gets blown up." Sergei's hand stayed in place.

"Go on!" Ivankov said, annoyed.

"How do I open it safely?" Sergei asked Rush.

"Damn it! Open the goddamn door!" Ivankov cried.

"You open it!" Sergei said to Ivankov.

Ivankov considered. He turned it Rush. "How do we open it safely?"

"Reach into my pocket and pull out my cell phone. Enter 'star 66.' It'll be safe to open the car then."

"Get it, Danzig," Ivankov directed one of his thugs. "Sergei, keep him covered."

Sergei gratefully moved toward Rush, keeping him covered with a Springfield XD-S while Danzig reached toward Rush's pocket.

Rush had worked his feet free from the belt about five minutes earlier, using Ivankov's constant beatings as a distraction. When they thought he was just convulsing from the pain of the blows to his kidneys, he was actually twisting and turning the belt tied around his feet. Now, when Danzig came close enough, he kicked him with a wicked blow to the jaw, sending him sprawling back. Hoisting himself by the arms, Rush wrapped his legs around Sergei's neck, choking him before he could react.

Ivankov raised his Glock. "Get out of the way, Sergei. Don't make me shoot through you."

Taking advantage of the distraction, Amelia grabbed the cattle prod off the table and shoved it into Ivankov's back. He screamed. She scrambled over him like a cat and grabbed his gun. Clutching it in her hands, she skittered across the table and fired it at Ivankov. She missed him, but it didn't look like a warning shot. She looked like she meant to kill him but didn't know how a gun worked. Ivankov froze.

"Get down on your knees!" she said.

Ivankov got down on his knees.

Recovering from the kick to his head, Danzig grabbed a Ruger from the pile of guns and raised it. Amelia saw him and turned to him. She fired, striking him in the chest and bringing him down in a heap. Surprised, she blinked a couple of times, like a child who had knocked over a tower of blocks by accident.

Ivankov took advantage of her shock by diving over the table and reaching for the Glock. Amelia jerked back and fired. Two fingers of Ivankov's right hand blew off in a mist of red. He stopped and stared at his maimed hand.

Rush released the limp Sergei from between his legs. He fell to the ground, dead or unconscious. Swinging his legs up and kicking against the ceiling, Rush tried to break the pipe his arms were chained to, the chains digging into his wrists, tearing the skin, causing blood to run down into his eyes.

Ivankov lay on the table, clutching his maimed hand, howling for all the world like Tarzan. Amelia could have used that distraction as an opportunity to come to Rush's aid. Instead, she ran to the car.

"How do I open the car?" she asked.

Rush took a breath. "Just open it."

She swung the door open. Nothing happened. She looked back at Rush. "Remind me not to play poker with you."

Hanging from the pipe, he gave the ceiling another kick. "A little help here," he said, his voice still muffled by the goddamned respirator. Amelia just crawled in the car and rummaged through the back seat.

Ivankov stopped howling, rolled off the table, and headed for the pile of weapons in the corner. He grabbed a Gewehr assault with his non-bloody hand.

Rush kicked the ceiling once more and the pipe finally burst loose from the concrete above it. Brownish water spilled from it as he fell to the ground, and the released, unconscious Guzman toppled on top of him.

Ivankov fumbled with the rifle, cursing because his damned trigger finger was missing.

Pushing Guzman off him, Rush struggled loose from the pipe. His hands were still chained together, but he drove himself toward Ivankov, using the chains as a weapon, wrapping them around the rifle and yanking it out of Ivankov's grasp. He twisted it to the side and brought his knee crashing into Ivankov's jaw.

Ivankov's head rocked back into the concrete wall with a sickening thud. His eyes clouded over and he collapsed like a rag doll. Rush took the Gewehr and considered emptying the clip into him. At times like this, he always thought the same thing: *What would Batman do?*

Rush looked back to the GTO. Amelia was still tearing at the back seat searching, presumably, for the flash drive. She turned to him.

"It's not here!"

"Not anymore," Rush said.

"You lied to him?!" she said, affronted. "Why?"

"I don't know. To protect you?"

"Stupid reason. I can take care of myself."

"What's on that flash drive, anyway?"

"Things."

"Why did you tell Ivankov *I* had it?"

"To stay alive. As long as he didn't have it, he had a reason not to kill me, right?"

Rush could see her point, but he was a little surprised that an eighteen-year-old girl could keep that thought in her head while going through what she was going through. But then this was no ordinary eighteen-year-old girl.

"I didn't think you'd drive it right up here!" she said. "That was wild." Then she paused, thoughtfully.

"Did he really kill my brother?"

Rush nodded.

Amelia went to the corner and pulled a Sig Sauer Mosquito twenty-two caliber out of the seemingly inexhaustible pile of weapons. She went up to Ivankov, his back against the wall, the red stain from his smashed skull staining the concrete.

She put the gun to his head.

"You don't want to do that," Rush said.

"Why not?"

"You don't want to spend the rest of your life in prison."

"You don't think I might get off for extenuating circumstances? I mean, look at me."

"Maybe," Rush said.

She moved the gun around and pointed it at Rush. "So where is it now?" she asked.

"What?"

"The flash drive, don't be stupid."

"The North Pole," Rush said. He'd found the flash drive the morning after he'd taken her home from the Nocturne. He hadn't known what it was, but he'd put it in a safe place. Just in case.

Rush sat down on the wooden table, suddenly feeling very weary. "Are you going to shoot me for it?"

She lowered the gun. "It's in your apartment, isn't it?"

Rush's phone started ringing in his pocket. Holding up one finger to gesture for her to wait a goddamn minute, he pulled it out and checked the caller ID.

"Hey, Donleavy," Rush said.

"Crush. They got Trask."

"Who did?" he replied, puzzled.

"Whoever's doing this! They snatched him. Is the girl safe?"

"Yeah, I...." He looked around toward Amelia. She was gone. There was no one in the room but him and a lot of unconscious, bleeding men.

"You take care of her," Donleavy said.

"I will," he said. He turned his head back toward where Amelia had been, but he didn't make it all the way. A gun butt smacked him on the forehead, and he was distracted by a crash of thunder and a flash of lightning.

TWENTY-EIGHT

When he opened his eyes, Rush found that Amelia was gone. So either she'd hit him or she'd been taken by the one who did. He sat up, intending to run downstairs and try to catch up with her, but he threw up instead. Checking his phone, he saw he'd had eighteen calls from Zerbe.

"There you are!" Zerbe said when Rush called him back. "I was starting to get worried."

"Is Doc Adams in?" Doc Adams was their next-door neighbor, a retired brain surgeon who spent his time doing pharm drugs, eating chocolate cake, and watching infomercials while encroaching Alzheimer's took him further and further away from reality. He had patched up Rush and his friends on numerous occasions without reporting it to the police, either out of tact or forgetfulness.

"I'll see. Is it bad?"

"You tell me."

"How long will you be?"

"How long will it take me to crawl there?"

Rush hung up and went to collect Guzman.

◎

Once Rush and Guzman had made it out onto Almadero Street, Rush realized this wasn't the best part of L.A. to hail a cab. He'd call Uber, but his account had been discontinued after he'd had a disagreement with one of the drivers. The disagreement involved Rush pulling the driver out through the front window, like a breech birth.

He decided it would be easier to steal a car. He opted for a late-model BMW, because he figured whoever could afford that car could afford another one. Instead of going through the trouble of popping the lock, he just chucked a piece of asphalt through the window and let the car alarm blare. Car alarms blended in with the scenery downtown. It took him about five minutes to hotwire the thing, because he had to stop every few seconds and try to refocus his eyes. He wondered if he had a concussion; wondered if he had something worse. Finally getting the engine started, he loaded Guzman, unconscious again, into the passenger seat and drove off.

He even remembered to call 911 for Ivankov and Sergei. Would Batman have done that?

Rush and Guzman rode in the elevator up to Rush's apartment, both of them sitting on the floor, watching the floors tick by.

"Are you still alive?" Rush asked Guzman, after he had been silent for too long.

"A little bit," Guzman replied, his eyes still shut. "Where are we going again?"

"The North Pole."

"Oh, good."

The elevator stopped and the doors slid open. Rush made it to his door and slipped the key in the lock. It was good to be home, he thought as he breached the threshold and Guzman came stumbling after him, clutching his wounded arm.

"Zerbe! Is Adams here yet?"

Zerbe didn't answer. He couldn't really, seeing as he was duct-taped to a chair, naked from the waist up, with a red ball gag in his mouth.

TWENTY-NINE

Fifteen minutes before that, Zerbe was out in the hall, knocking on Doc Adams's door and trying to make him understand that he wasn't Adams's son, who, Zerbe believed, had died in a car accident in 2010.

"Jack? Is that you?"

"No, it's Zerbe, your next-door neighbor."

"Jack, I haven't got time for you and your faggot friends."

"It's Zerbe, Doc. Jack's...not here."

"Have you stopped hanging around with those fairies?"

"Yes. Yes, I have."

"I don't believe you. You're gonna catch the AIDS, you know that, don't you?"

"I'll be careful. Listen, a friend of mine is here. He needs help."

"I bet he's a fairy."

"No, no, he's not. He's K. C. Zerbe."

"Casey? Sounds like a queer."

"Well, he's not. He has a couple of friends coming over who need tending to."

The locks began to turn. The door opened. Doc Adams stood there, stark naked. Not in bad shape for a man in his seventies, but still, naked.

"Zerbe?" he asked.

"Yeah. Your son just left."

"My son died in a car accident on the Pacific Coast Highway."

"That's right."

"Him and his lover."

"That's right."

"I'm *for* gay marriage now."

"Do you want to put some pants on, Doc?"

He looked down at his waist.

"Son of a gun. I put 'em on yesterday."

"You gotta put them on every day. That's one of those things you got to do."

"Your friends, are they here now?"

"No, they're on their way."

"Bullet wounds?"

"I think so."

"How long till they get here?"

"Ten minutes?"

"That should give me enough time to find my pants."

The door closed. Zerbe could hear Doc calling out, "Hey, Jack, where are my pants?"

Zerbe sighed. Old age was for shit. He hoped he died young. But not too young.

He had just made it to his own door when the elevator opened and a young woman stepped out into the dimly lit hall. As the doors slid shut, he saw another figure hanging back, going to another floor. It was an unusual amount of traffic for this building after midnight.

The young woman came up to him.

"Amelia?" he asked.

It wasn't quite the face he'd seen before. It was battered and bruised, but more than that, it had changed internally. It had aged a few years.

"Is Crush here?" she asked.

"No. How did you get away?"

She started to answer...then she fainted. Dead away. She actually collapsed in his arms. Zerbe thought women only did that in the movies.

He jostled her a few times to see if she was kidding, then he dragged her inside the apartment like an awkward piece of furniture. How did the guys in the movies always do this so gracefully? Zerbe wondered this as he hauled her across the threshold and dumped her, half on the sofa, half on the floor.

He hoisted her legs up onto the cushions and got an old Lakers fleece blanket to cover her. Then he sat down on the sofa himself, winded. He really had to get in better shape. He made a note to himself to put that on his list of things to do. After he learned to fly a hang glider and write that screenplay for Quentin Tarantino.

Looking over at her, he wondered how the hell she

got here. And where was Caleb? And why did she think he would be here before her? And what the hell had happened to her?

"Zerbe?" she said, her eyes still closed. "That's a silly name. It sounds like a villain in a sci-fi movie. 'Zerbe, tell the Alliance that resistance is futile.' That's funny."

"Where's Rush?"

"He got held up. He sent me ahead. Said you'd take care of me."

Zerbe was glad Rush said that. "Should I call somebody?" he asked. "Your father?" Zerbe wanted to take the words back as soon as they came out of his mouth. Amelia's father had been grabbed, he remembered. And this didn't seem the best time to tell her about it. "Let me get you some water first."

Crossing to the kitchenette, he pulled out his cell phone and filled a Bullwinkle jam-jar glass with water from the tap. He started to call Donleavy, but then thought maybe he should call Rush first. He hesitated.

Then he looked up at Amelia. She was standing in the middle of the room.

"Give me the phone," she said. Her hand was outstretched toward him, but Zerbe wasn't looking at that. She had pulled her shirt off and was naked from the waist up. She had the kind of breasts Zerbe hadn't seen for a long while. The kind that weren't on a computer screen. He was entranced. He gave her the phone. She tossed it onto the sofa.

"What did you do that for?"

"I don't want you to call my father. Not yet."

"No, I don't mean that." Zerbe gestured toward her shirt, which was balled up on the sofa. "That."

She moved to him and kissed him. This struck Zerbe as odd. Why would a girl who had just been through some sort of traumatic experience want to kiss a relative stranger? And a relative stranger like Zerbe?

There were a lot of red flags that should have told Zerbe to put the brakes on right then, be a gentleman, tuck her in, and make her some warm soup. But on the other hand, he hadn't been laid for approximately two years and six months.

So he kissed her back.

In the long run, once he was tied to that chair with the ball gag in his mouth and the gun pressed to his head, he knew he should have regretted it. But he didn't really.

They were nice kisses.

THIRTY

A glob of drool, glistening in the dim light, dropped from the red ball in Zerbe's mouth.

Rush spun around on his heel but he was too late. Amelia and Stanley Trask stood behind him, blocking his way to the door, which was still ajar, offering freedom just out of reach. Trask held a Browning twenty-two in his hand. Amelia stood next to him, a petulant expression on her pretty face.

"Why didn't you ever call me, Tony?" she said to Guzman, who didn't answer. He just collapsed on the sofa as if he were a Macy's parade balloon with all the gas released.

Rush pried the ball gag from Zerbe's mouth, noticing as he did that Zerbe was naked from the waist up and that Amelia was wearing Zerbe's Green Lantern shirt. What had gone on here?

"You okay?" he asked Zerbe after the gag came out with a syrupy slurping sound.

"Sorry. She came here. Said you sent her. Then that

one showed up," Zerbe said, glaring at Trask.

"He tied you up?"

"No, she did. Before he got here. It sounded like fun at the time."

Shaking his head, Rush started to pull the tape off Zerbe's arms.

"That's all right," Trask barked. "Leave him be." He looked at Guzman coldly. "We have things to discuss."

Guzman spoke up from the sofa. "Mr. Trask, we can't do this here."

"I think we can," Trask replied, calmly.

"Let me guess," Rush said to Guzman. "This is another one of those thing you're not proud of?"

Guzman sat up as if he wanted to explain. "Crush, I—" he started, but Trask gestured to him with his gun, and he stopped short.

"What are you going to do, Trask?" Rush asked. "Kill all of us?"

"Well, I only really want to kill him," Trask gestured to Guzman, "but you'll have to go along for the ride."

"Daddy!" Amelia cried out, horrified.

"Stanley," Guzman objected, "we had a deal—"

"Kitten, be quiet and listen to you father for once!" Trask snapped at his daughter, ignoring Guzman.

He took a deep breath and addressed Guzman: "You're a hard man to track down, do you know that?"

Amelia threw herself on top of Guzman. He cried out in pain as she rubbed her body against his wound.

"Don't, Daddy! You said you were doing this so

Tony and I could be together!"

"He's a blackmailer, Amelia," Trask said. "And a child molester."

"Come on, Papa! It wasn't like that!"

"It was exactly like that."

Amelia was screaming now, "I won't let you hurt him!"

Trask waved his gun, exasperated. "Fine. Throw a tantrum. I'll still be here when you're done."

The faced each other in silence. A standoff.

Rush took advantage of the pause to ask Amelia a question. "Why did you tell me Guzman killed your uncle?"

She shrugged. "I thought if you were mad at him, you might tell me where he was. Or go track him down." Amelia turned to Guzman and gave him a little snuggle. "I figured if anybody could find you, Crush could."

Guzman just sunk back into the sofa, like he wished he were somewhere else.

Still taped to his chair, Zerbe spoke up. "Anybody want to tell me what's going on?"

Trask laughed. "The funny thing is, I'm actually tempted to tell you. To explain it all. I always thought it was idiotic in movies when the villain stopped to explain everything instead of just shooting somebody. Now I understand. It's a delaying tactic." He paused, his hand flexing on the gun. "This is rather hard to do."

Guzman pushed Amelia off of him and leaned toward Trask, pleading, "Mr. Trask, I swear I won't—"

Trask shot Guzman in the head.

Guzman fell back on the sofa, dead. He didn't have time to look surprised.

Amelia screamed.

Trask sighed, looking very tired. "It is very hard," he said. Then he pointed the gun at Rush. "And I don't think it's going to get any easier."

Amelia clutched Guzman's body to her breast, crying like a baby. Rush prepared for the impact of the bullet.

Then the front door swung open and a dark figure appeared, backlit by the hallway light.

Trask glanced toward the door for a second, and that was all Rush needed. He grabbed Trask's gun hand and swung it aside, driving his body, elbow first, into Trask's breastbone. Pivoting his elbow up, he cracked Trask's jaw, wrenching the gun out of his hand and pushing him, driving him hard against the wall.

Grabbing the samurai sword from its display rack on the wall, Rush whipped around and pressed the point against Trask's throat.

At the apartment door, Frida Morales stood looking at the scene, stunned.

"Frida, darling!" Zerbe said, from his chair. "What took you so long?"

Rush shot a curious look at Zerbe from the corner of his eye, and Zerbe lifted his leg, exposing his ankle—the electronic tether on it was busted, wires exposed.

"It broke after Amelia tied me up. It was like

sending my Frida the Bat Signal."

Zerbe laughed, like a giddy child, then shut up when he realized that Amelia was still holding onto Guzman, weeping. Not the time for levity. Frida stepped into the room and peered at the dead man.

"What happened?" she asked.

Trask answered quickly, his eyes still locked with Rush's. "I killed my brother. Drowned him in my pool." He looked down at Guzman. "That man found the body. He tried to blackmail me. So I shot him."

Rush met his stare.

"Call the police, Frida."

THIRTY-ONE

Rush stood next to Trask by the big window, looking down at the night and the city. A police car, siren flashing, slowly made its way down Wilshire, inching through the gridlocked traffic.

"I can't believe how long it's taking them to get here," Trask said, breaking the long silence.

"It just feels that way," Rush replied.

"Yeah. My last moments of freedom. I should be having a steak at the Palm. Not standing here with you."

Rush shifted his weight on his tired feet. "It doesn't add up," he said. "Guzman wouldn't dive into that pool. He couldn't swim."

"It was the shallow end."

"And he never had that flash drive. Amelia had it."

Trask didn't say anything. Just kept staring at the city.

"She killed your brother," Rush said. "To protect Guzman. She knew if Walter went to the feds, he'd go down with everyone else."

Trask stared ahead in silence.

"That's what Guzman saw, isn't it? That's how he was blackmailing you."

Trask shut his eyes. "She's just a little girl. She thought she loved him." He looked over at the sofa. Amelia was asleep, looking younger than Rush had ever seen her. Guzman's sheet-covered body was next to her. She looked like a child sleeping with her teddy bear.

"So you admit it?" Rush asked.

Trask looked back at the city with no expression on his Gill-Man face. "I killed my brother."

"You can't—"

"Do you listen to country music, Mr. Rush?"

"Sometimes."

"That's my story and I'm sticking to it."

Trask stared out at the skyline, a thin smile playing over his face. "Oh and Mr. Rush?"

"Yeah?"

"Where is that damned flash drive?"

"The North Pole," Rush replied, pointing to the glass panel on the ceiling where Zerbe had projected the satellite image of the Earth. The flash drive was taped to the back of the glass, right above the North Pole.

"Ah," said Trask, "so you weren't lying after all."

"I never lie about important things," Rush said.

◎

Eleven months later, Rush walked across his apartment to Zerbe's computer console, eating a bowl of Sugar Smacks, his usual late-evening snack. There was an email from Donleavy saying that Trask had been sentenced to twenty years for his brother Walter's murder. Rush sighed. Justice.

Gail and Zerbe were nearby, shooting pool. Rush figured he'd wait for them to finish the game before he told them. Gail still limped a little, but other than that, her recovery was amazing. She'd beat Rush in a sparring match last week, and he hadn't even let her win. Gail was a real superhero, he decided. So was Zerbe, for that matter. He deserved to wear his Green Lantern shirt. They should start a Justice League for broken-down heroes.

Rush looked back at the computer. He clicked on the picture menu and brought up the photo of Amelia in the club, the one she'd taken of herself the night they met.

Call him crazy, but even after all she'd done, Rush still liked her. Hell, he liked Trask, too. Trask may have been a slimy crook and a killer, but when it came to it, he took a murder rap for his daughter because he loved her. And Amelia killed her uncle because she loved Guzman. Everything they did, they did for love.

Rush moved the mouse, rolling the cursor over the picture, wondering if maybe that was why he kept looking at her. Because he couldn't imagine loving someone that much. He guessed that ought to make him feel superior to them. Smarter. But he hardly ever felt smart anymore.

He rolled the cursor to the task bar.

Well, there's one thing computers have over the human brain, Rush thought as he dragged the picture to the trash and hit "delete." *Wouldn't it be nice if we could do that.*

Get ready for more Crush action!
A preview of the next book by Phoef Sutton

HEART ATTACK & VINE

A Crush Novel

April 2013

"I hate L.A.," Layla said as she traced a thin black line with her paintbrush onto the cool, white tile that lined the face of the Feingold's Deli stall in the bustling Grand Central Market. "What I love is Los Angeles."

She pronounced it with a hard "g," the way people did in the 1930s. "Los Ang-a-lees." With her short-cropped hair, bleached a platinum blond, and her white blouse, Layla looked like she could have been an extra in an old gangster movie herself. Only the Bluetooth headset clipped to her ear spoiled the illusion.

"I hate the new Hollywood Boulevard. It's almost as bad as Times Square in New York. And I hate what they're doing to Los Feliz and West Hollywood and all the faux-hip shops in Silver Lake," she said as she painted graffiti on the front of Feingold's. "What I love is Downtown Los Angeles, in all its messy glory."

Caleb Rush was sitting at a table in front of the Sticky Rice stall, munching on a mess of smelly fried smelt with dipping sauce, Bluetooth nestled in his ear, chatting with Layla over the airwaves, watching her from the corner of his eye so as not to make it too apparent that they were talking to each other. Layla was paying good coin for Rush to keep an eye on her, and that's what Rush was doing.

"God, I hate hipsters," Layla said with a sigh. "They're ruining this town."

Rush grunted an agreement while he half-watched her trace retro-style sketches of deli sandwiches on Feingold's façade—graffiti art, only made to order.

Layla Lowenstein was in her early thirties. With her black eyeliner, blue nail polish, and the tattoo of Felix the Cat that peeked from the sleeve of her vintage blouse, she was a poster child for the hipster generation. No one hates hipsters more than hipsters, Rush thought.

Layla was a part-time artist, part-time actress, and part-time grifter. There was nothing full-time about her.

"We're the last of a dying breed, Crush," she said, using the nickname by which he was best known.

"What breed is that?" he asked.

"Hired guns."

"I don't use a gun."

"Neither do I," Layla said. "I meant it metaphorically. My guns are my brushes. My guns are my way with words. Oh, and my dark, mysterious eyes. Those are my guns, too."

"Okay," Rush said, just to pass the time. "What are my guns?"

"Your guns are you, Crush. You're your own guns."

Rush dipped some more fish into the spicy sauce and took in his surroundings. Grand Central Market was the innards of Los Angeles. The stomach and lower intestines of the town. A city block sandwiched between the faded glory of the Million Dollar Theatre and Mexican shops that sell votive candles and statues of saints. Recently renovated, the market had, housed under one roof, dozens of stalls featuring everything anyone would want to eat, drink, or ingest. There were delis frequented by thirty-year-old Jews in fedoras and taco stands where Mexican immigrants actually ate. There were stalls that sold traditional Chinese medicine, kept in dusty vials that looked like they had been there since the turn of the last century. There were trendy hot spots for trendy hipsters, like kombucha bars and artisanal chocolate shops.

On one side was Broadway, not the bustling Broadway of New York but the run-down, seedy Broadway of L.A. On the other side, the market opened onto Bunker Hill and the funicular railway called Angel's Flight, whose slanted cars took the trip up the steep route to California Plaza and the swooping walls of Disney Hall—that is, when they weren't closed for safety reasons, which they usually were.

"Mark my words, Crush," Layla said. "In three years all the old, dirty, sleazy storefronts in this place are going to be gone, and there'll be nothing but latte shops, organic cheeses, and pressed-juice stands. It's the way of the world."

Someone walking through the crowded aisles between the stalls caught Rush's eye and made the hair on his arms stand up. It wasn't that the man was particularly threatening. He was tall and slender, with neatly groomed hair, a gray sportcoat, and an attaché case, like a time traveler from the sixties. The way he looked around with hooded eyes, as if he was a predator seeking prey, sent a warning signal to Rush.

"Principal is approaching," Rush said into his headset with practiced calmness.

Layla got excited. "Groovy," she said, putting her brush in a jar of water on the counter and waiting for the man to come up to her. "Meet you back at my apartment." She pulled the Bluetooth from her ear.

Rush reached in the pocket of his black hoodie and checked the envelope Layla had given him. He didn't know what was in it. He wasn't being paid to know; he was just being paid to make the transfer. Getting up and throwing the leavings of the fried fish away, he walked over to the deli stand and made as if he was looking at the little blackboard with the daily specials, pointedly ignoring Layla, who stood next to him, washing out her brushes and singing "California Dreaming" softly to herself.

Sportcoat sidled up to Layla and backed her into the counter in a way that was both casual and threatening.

"Hello, Bridget."

So Layla was "Bridget" to Sportcoat. Interesting. She was Layla Lowenstein, but he'd always doubted that was her real name. A girl like Layla made up a new identity to fit every occasion.

"Do you have it?" Sportcoat said, letting his brief-case thud like a pendulum against the deli counter.

Rush came up to Sportcoat and tapped him on the shoulder. Not in a particularly aggressive way. Caleb Rush was six-foot-five, two hundred and fifty pounds of muscle in a tight black T-shirt and hoodie. His clean-shaven head had a nasty scar running from above his left eye across his skull. He didn't have to act aggres-sively. His physical presence was threat enough.

"You're not dealing with her," Rush said. "You're dealing with me. I have what you want."

Sportcoat looked at Rush and tried very hard not to look intimidated. "That wasn't part of the deal," he said, reaching into his jacket pocket and putting his hand on an object that Rush thought might be a gun.

"It's part of the deal now," Rush said in an even tone. "Come on." If Sportcoat had a gun, that meant he was expecting trouble, but he'd have been expecting trouble from Layla, not from a mean piece of a work like Rush.

As he often did, Rush wondered what the hell he had gotten himself into. He was a part-timer himself, and one of his trades was doing odd jobs for friends. Layla was one of those friends. She'd asked him to handle the transfer of an unnamed object to an unnamed buyer. Layla was infamous for her transactions, usually of stolen or illegally obtained merchandise. Rush had no moral objections to Layla's deals, legitimate or otherwise. She was a friend, and her money was good. End of story.

But the first thing he had to do was get Sportcoat away from Layla and out of this crowd of people. If Sportcoat was going to use his gun, Rush wanted him alone, with no bystanders, innocent or otherwise. He turned and walked through the crowd, not looking back to see if Sportcoat was following. Rush was willing him away.

Walking to a little side exit tucked between a cheese store and a coffee shop, Rush pushed through a door and into a small hallway lit by a flickering fluorescent fixture. The hallway felt small and dingy after the roomy cacophony of the market. He heard footsteps clicking behind him. A man's steps. Crossing to another door, Rush swung it open and entered a dark corridor. Its walls were covered with red floral wallpaper, faded and peeling, a relic of a gaudier, flashier past. They had entered the neighboring building, the illustrious Million Dollar Theatre.

Built in 1918 by Sid Grauman and designed by Albert Martin, it was L.A.'s first grand movie palace. A mad mix of Spanish Colonial and Churrigueresque fantasy, it had stood for nearly a hundred years, doing service as a movie theater, a jazz club, a Mexican vaudeville house, and a Spanish-language church. Now it stood empty, waiting for a savior or a wrecking ball.

Walking through the dark wings of the theater, Rush headed onto the stage in front of the tattered movie screen. His way was lit by a ghost light—a single bulb in a small wire cage set on a pole in the middle of the stage. Ghost lights were a theatrical tradition, an offering to the twin show-business deities of superstition and safety.

The theater was inky dark and silent, a cathedral to the business of motion-picture exhibition. The vast expanse of seats lay before Rush like an unexplored cavern, and the proscenium rose high above him. Longhorn skulls and Aztec gods stared down from the ornate arch. Rush walked several steps past the ghost light and turned around.

Sportcoat was standing about ten feet away from him. The ghost light stood between them like an umpire at a prizefight. "Are we there yet?" Sportcoat asked.

"Yes," Rush said. "Do you have the money?"

"Not so fast. Let's get acquainted first. What do they call you?"

"Busy," Rush said. "Let's get this done."

"Okay, Busy," Sportcoat said. "Mr. Cleveland just calls me 'Bub.'"

Mr. Cleveland? He said the name as if Rush should be familiar with it. He didn't know Rush was just a hired intermediary, and Rush wasn't about to clue him in.

"All right, Bub." Unzipping his hoodie, Rush pulled

out the package. It was a plain manila envelope, flat and unimpressive. "Do you have the money or not?"

"I have it." Bub set the briefcase down on the wooden stage. "Shall we count to three and push?"

"Do we really have to?"

"Mr. Cleveland is fond of ceremony."

"All right," Rush said, crouching down and placing the envelope on the stage. "One, two, three."

Rush slid the envelope across to Bub, and Bub slid the briefcase to Rush. Rush opened it and saw that it was filled with bundles of twenty-dollar bills. A lot of bundles. There must have been a hundred thousand dollars in there. Layla was only paying Rush five hundred to make this exchange. His roommate was right—he really had to start being a better businessman.

He looked up to see Bub examining the contents of the envelope Rush had given him. "Doesn't seem worth it," he said. "But like Grandma used to say, it takes all kinds of crazy people to make a crazy world."

"Your grandma was a smart woman," Rush said.

"You wouldn't say that if you met my grandpa."

Rush shut the briefcase and stood up. The transaction was complete. No gunplay had been necessary. Rush considered that a success.

"Now," Rush said, "I leave first. You follow."

"Whatever you say."

It didn't really make any difference who led and who followed, but Rush knew that it did matter that he stayed in charge. He walked, covering the distance between them in firm, steady strides. A thought occurred to him when he was opposite the ghost light. He stopped, set the briefcase down on the stage, and opened it.

The bundles of cash looked impressive. He picked one up and flipped through it, like a magician rifling through a deck of cards. The top two bills were real American money. The rest of the bundle was made of real Monopoly money.

He glanced up at Bub. And at the gun in his hand.

"You had to look, didn't you?" Bub asked.

"I really did. Was this your idea or Mr. Cleveland's?" Rush gestured to the play money.

"Mr. Cleveland thought it would be funny. Bridget called him Mr. Moneybags."

"Bridget has a way with words."

"I'm going to walk away," Bub said. "You're not going to follow me. Is that understood?"

"Of course. There's no need anyway."

Bub turned to walk off. Then he turned back. "What do you mean?"

"You know Bridget," Rush said. "If Mr. Cleveland cheated her, don't you think she planned on cheating him?"

Bub eyed Rush. "Go on."

"Do you really think that's the genuine article you have in your hand?" Rush had no idea what the genuine article was, of course, but he was pretty sure that whatever Layla was selling was fake. It was just her way.

Bub maneuvered the manila envelope open again and looked at the contents. Rush could see that they looked like old government documents, and they were marked with a rubber stamp in red ink. Bub licked his thumb and rubbed one of the red markings. His thumb left a bloody red smear.

"It's a fake!" he said, affronted.

"That's fake. These are fake," Rush said, pointing to the bundles in the attaché case. "We're even."

"I don't think Mr. Cleveland will see it that way," Bub said. "You picked the wrong man to fuck with."

"I didn't pick anybody. I'm just a delivery man."

"We both know better than that." Bub walked closer and kicked the attaché case closed. "Pick it up for me."

"There's a couple hundred real dollars in here," Rush said. "Don't I get to keep that?"

"Shut up," he said, gesturing with the gun. "You're lucky I don't shoot you right now."

Rush latched the attaché case and handed it to Bub, who leaned forward to take it. When he bent down, Rush grabbed the ghost light and smashed it on his head. The light bulb burst and the theater went black, but Rush didn't need to see. He grasped Bub where he knew his wrist was and twisted it back. Bub hissed in pain and slammed the back of his head hard into Rush's face.

Rush took the force of the blow, stumbled back, and then gripped Bub's wrist more tightly and twisted it.

He heard a satisfying crunch as the joint snapped. Bub groaned, and his gun discharged in a loud explosion off into the wings. Rush spun Bub around, stepped back, and delivered a kick to his chest.

By now, Rush's eyes had adjusted to the dark, and he could make out shapes and shadows. He could just see Bub flying back and falling off the stage into the greater blackness beyond. Pulling his iPhone from the back pocket of his jeans, he switched on the flashlight app and located the attaché case where it lay on the stage. Next to it was the envelope Layla had given him. He picked them both up and walked to the edge of the stage.

He shined the light on the floor in front of the stage, where Bub lay clutching his arm and moaning. The gun was next to him, but he didn't seem to be aware of it. He opened his eyes and looked up at the flashlight. "What the hell is your problem?"

"I was hired to make an exchange," Rush said, tossing the envelope down at him. "Now I've made it. Take care of yourself." He turned off the flashlight and exited, stage right.

◎

Rush walked around the side of the building on Third Street, let himself into the little lobby, and stepped onto the elevator. It was a small one, having been installed in the seventies when the building was remodeled. In the 1910s it had been the home of the Department of Water & Power. Back then L.A. was just another city in California.

He rode up to the fourteenth floor, walked to an apartment door, and pressed the little black buzzer on the door. Layla opened the door.

"Well?" she said. "Did you get the cash?" Since he'd seen her, she had dyed her hair a bright red and was drying it with a towel.

"Yes and no," Rush said, walking in. The apartment was small but elaborately furnished. The walls were inlaid with wooden cabinets, and the light fixtures were made of elaborate stained glass. "Nice place," he said.

"It used to be William Mulholland's office, back in the day."

"What day was that?" Rush said, sitting on a horsehair sofa and setting the attaché case on an old coffee table.

"The bad old days," she said. "Mulholland is the guy who stole water so Los Angeles could grow. In 1918. It's a city founded by pirates, Crush." She tossed her towel on a love seat. "You want a beer? Or a hard cider? Everybody's drinking hard cider now."

"What did they drink in the bad old days?"

"Bootlegged Scotch, I guess."

"Got any of that?"

"Only the real kind."

"I guess that'll have to do." Rush opened the case. The bundles of cash looked glorious.

"Hot damn," Layla said.

"Don't get too excited," he said, tossing a bundle to her. She flipped through it. "That bastard."

"You were cheating him," Rush said.

"Yes, but I'm the underdog. They always root for the underdog."

"Who does?"

"The audience."

Rush rubbed his big bald head with his big hand. "Layla, there's no audience. This isn't a play or a movie."

Layla shrugged. "In my mind, it's all a movie. I'm the lead. A Manic Pixie Dream Girl who muddles through life by her wits and her charm, conning rich bad guys out of their ill-gotten gains and winning the heart of the Hunky Good-hearted Bodyguard Action Hero."

"Who's going to play you?"

Layla looked offended. "Me, of course. They're holding out for Zooey Deschanel, but I think she's too old. The Rock will play you, of course."

"I'd prefer Vin Diesel. Who am I?"

"You're the bodyguard, stupid."

"I don't recall you winning my heart."

"Well, we have to work a romance into it. Give the audience what it wants."

"What if you're not the heroine? What if you're the villain?"

"An anti-heroine?" She shook her head. "Sounds like a seventies movie. Directed by Sidney Lumet or somebody like that. Not very current."

"What were you supposed to be selling to him?"

She smiled a bright charming smile. "Letters of transit."

"I need more."

"Movie memorabilia is a big collectible item these days. You know, the ruby slippers from *The Wizard of Oz*. The black bird from *The Maltese Falcon*. Rosebud from *Citizen Kane*. Have you seen any of these movies, Crush?"

"I go to the Cinematheque occasionally."

"Have you seen *Casablanca*?"

"'We'll always have Paris.'"

"That's the one. Do you remember the letters of transit? The secret documents that Peter Lorre gave Humphrey Bogart and Bogart gave Ingrid Bergman so she could leave Casablanca at the end?"

"You forgot to say 'spoiler alert.'"

"After seventy years you get a pass," she said. "Anyway, I'm selling the original prop." She opened a drawer in her coffee table, took out ten envelopes, and laid them on the table. "The original letters of transit." She took out a Marlboro Light and lit it with a match that she scraped against the tile fireplace.

"Those things will kill you," Rush said.

"A lot of things will kill me. Anyway, I sold them to three collectors yesterday. I've got six more on the hook."

Rush looked at the envelopes. "Are any of them real?"

Layla looked at Rush as if he'd just said he believed in Santa Claus.

"Honey, there are no real letters of transit. It was just a plot device the screenwriters made up. It's all pretend."

"But are any of them the original prop from the movie?"

She considered for a moment then opened another drawer. "These two. One was for long shots. The other one is the gold mine. What they call the hero prop. The one for close-ups." She took a long, thin envelope, weathered and stained and marked CONFIDENTIAL SECRET. Undoing the flap on top, she slid out two pieces of paper covered in typewritten French and marked with various official-looking stamps. "It's glorious. A real piece of the dream. Worth maybe a hundred thousand."

"Where did you get it?"

"I borrowed it."

"You stole it."

"Stealing involves keeping. I borrowed it from a collector. A very nice old man who lives in the Hollywood hills."

"Did this borrowing involve breaking and entering?"

"Maybe," she admitted. "But I'll 'break and enter' it back. I needed it to make these copies." She opened one of the other envelopes and pulled out a nearly identical copy. "Pretty good, huh? I arranged to sell it nine times over."

"You should have used higher-quality ink. It smeared."

Layla started. "Shit. Does he know?"

"Bub? Yes. I imagine Mr. Cleveland knows by now."

"Well, shoot," she said. She got up and started collecting her things. "I wanted to sell those other six before anybody found out."

"So now what are you going to do?"

"Disappear. Move to another city. Change my name."

"You think that will be enough? Mr. Cleveland sounds like a dangerous man."

"He's rich and he's crazy and his name's not Cleveland."

"What is his name?"

She looked at Rush like she was thinking something over. Then she picked up the real letters of transit and handed them to him. "Take these."

"I thought you were going to return them."

"Change of plan," she said. "Just keep them safe. You'll hear from me in two years."

"Why two years?"

"Because that's what it always says: 'Two years later.' Right after the dissolve. That's when you find out what happens to the heroine."

"The Manic Pixie Dream Girl?"

"That's right. When she goes off to find herself. Without the letters of transit or any evidence to tie her down." She pulled her car keys out of her pocket. "Do you want a Mini Cooper?"

"You don't need a car?"

"Not where I'm heading. It makes a better story. 'She arrived in New York with nothing but the clothes on her back and twenty dollars in her purse.' "

"And how much in the lining of her jacket?"

"A couple hundred thou. But that'll be our little secret." She grabbed her jacket. "Take care of yourself, Crush. When you see me again, I'll be on top of the world."

Layla kissed him on the head and was gone, leaving the door of the apartment wide open. She didn't care. She wasn't coming back.

Rush thought of her occasionally over the next few months. When he heard of an unidentified dead body being discovered in the Angeles National Forest, he wondered if it might be her. He told K. C. Zerbe, his roommate and half-brother, to search for her occasionally on the internet.

"But you don't know her real name," Zerbe said. "That makes it difficult. Or impossible."

So Rush just kept the letter of transit hidden in a wall in his loft and didn't think about Layla much. Two Christmases rolled by, and two New Years. The crowd at the Nocturne drank and danced and aged two years under Rush's watchful eye. It was January, and the Oscar nominations were the hot topic, everyone calling up the list on their mobile devices and discussing which of the movies they'd seen and which they'd only heard about. Rush, standing against the wall and being invisible like a good bouncer, hadn't seen or heard of any of them. He didn't keep in touch with pop culture.

One of the nightclubbers shoved her oversize cell phone in front of his nose and asked him what he thought. He was about to shrug and say he didn't think about it much at all when he saw the Best Supporting Actress nomination for an up-and-coming star named Amanda Fairchild. Take away her black hair and her blue eyes and she was a dead ringer for Layla.

Once a con artist, always a con artist, thought Rush.

TO BE CONTINUED

ABOUT THE AUTHOR

Phoef Sutton is a novelist, television writer, and playwright whose work has won two Emmys, a Peabody, a Writers Guild Award, a GLAAD Award, and a Television Academy Honors Award. He was an executive producer of *Cheers*, a writer/producer for such shows as *Boston Legal* and *NewsRadio*, a writer for *Terriers*, and the creator of several TV shows, including the cult hit *Thanks*.

On the book front, Sutton co-authored the new mystery *Wicked Charms* with Janet Evanovich, and he's collaborating on a new series with Evanovich that will launch in 2016. His other novels include the romantic thriller *15 Minutes to Live*, and he is the co-author of a new serialized novel, *The Dead Man*. Sutton lives with his family in South Pasadena, California.